TURLOUGH McKEV

THE TAOISEACH'S COAT

Blackwater Press

To The Real Mary

© Copyright text: Turlough McKevitt.

First published in 1996 by BLACKWATER PRESS, Unit 7/8, Broomhill Business Park, Dublin 24.

Printed at the press of the publishers.

All rights reserved. No part of this publication may be reproduced, stored in a retrieval system, or transmitted in any form, or by any means, electronic, mechanical, photocopying, recording, or otherwise, without the prior written permission of the publishers.

This book is subject to the conditions that it shall not, by way of trade or otherwise, be lent, re-sold, hired out or otherwise circulated without the publisher's prior consent in any form of binding or cover other than that in which it is published and without a similar condition being imposed on the subsequent purchaser.

ISBN: 0 86121 807 8
British Library Catloguing-in-Publication Data.
A catalogue record for this book is available from the British Library.
McKevitt, Turlough, The Taoiseach's Coat.
Editor: Deirdre Whelan
Assistant Editor: Zoë O'Connor
Cover design/illustration: Turlough McKevitt
Layout: M & J Graphics Ltd.

– Contents –

CHAPTER	PAGE
Preface	4
1. The Taoiseach's Troubles	6
2. A Stranger in Torn Tights	13
3. Plans and Plots	20
4. Tales, Wails, Moans and Bones	25
5. The Plot Thickens…	30
6. Paste and Papering	34
7. Fears and Firkin	39
8. Garrett's Well	44
9. Hide and Seek	49
10. The Cavern	54
11. Terrorist Tactics	63
12. The Time, The Time…	69
13. Lights, Cameras, Action!	75
14. A Terrible Time…	86
15. Night Frights	92
16. Meanwhile, Back at the Cave…	104
17. Waterworks	108
18. We'll All Go	112
19. Breakout	119
20. Granny to the Rescue	123
21. Hearts and Minds	128
22. All's Well	140

Preface

On a bright moonlight night in mid spring, a hungry badger, rooting for grubs, dislodged a loose stone from the side of a grassy hill. It rolled away, and the badger, unconcerned, ambled on in his search for food. The stone had covered a hole that allowed air to flow into a dark cavern built under the hill. All remained dark inside until the moon rose a little higher in the sky. The moonlight reached the opening and trickled along the air vent until it pierced the darkness inside. It moved across dark sleeping forms until it rested on a seated figure on a heavy ornate chair.

The glimmer of light disturbed the sleeper.

He opened one eye and looked around. He couldn't tell what had awakened him. He could see little in the dimness but was reassured by the sound of gentle snoring all around. As the moon rose higher the beam of light retreated down the steps which led up to the sleeper's chair and then across the sleeping forms until it vanished back through the opening. The cave was again plunged into gloom. The sleeper was fully awake now.

"Is it the time?" he whispered. The only reply was the sound of gentle snoring.

CHAPTER ONE

The Taoiseach's Troubles

The moon shone on the surrounding countryside outside the cave. Far away, it also beamed down on the ever-busy city. Its brilliance was only outdone by the powerful floodlights in the courtyard of government buildings. They washed the giant clock dome with a strong golden light that made the moonlight itself look sickly.

A telephone rang in the Taoiseach's office where he and his secretary, The Nod, were working late into the night. The floor of their office, every desk, chair and any available surface was covered with letters of every size, shape and colour. The Taoiseach looked bothered as he glanced at the phone.

"Don't answer it, Nod," he barked, "it's probably that dreadful woman again. How she got my direct telephone number, I'll never know!"

The Nod knew, of course, but said nothing.

"Hello," he answered, to the Taoiseach's annoyance. "It's the Lord Mayor," he said. "He wishes to remind you about the National Parade."

"How could I forget the National Parade?" the Taoiseach almost roared. "After the mess somebody made of it last year," he added, looking meaningfully at The Nod.

The Taoiseach always attended the National Parade, an event of great importance. Every year, towns and industries throughout the country sent floats and bands to parade through the streets of the capital city. The Taoiseach usually sat in the front seat of the viewing stand where he could be seen by the crowds and television cameras. Dressed in his best coat he would nod, bow and wave at the passing floats.

Last year, to his surprise, the Taoiseach had found himself sandwiched between a visiting ballet dancer who could speak only Russian and a mime artist who waved his hands a lot. To make matters worse, a very large visiting Italian opera singer had been put sitting directly in front of him. His view was blocked and in order to be seen by the camera, he had to shift over and back. The mime artist and the ballet dancer thought he was starting a Mexican wave and joined in the fun. Everybody else on the stand joined in. The nation watched in

amusement as the VIPs all Mexican-waved together. The sudden movement caused the scaffolding under the stand to shift. With a "crack" it collapsed throwing the celebrities into a large jumble. Fortunately nobody was hurt but the newspapers agreed that the country expected public figures to behave in a more dignified way and they hoped that the Taoiseach would give a better lead in the future.

Curiously, The Nod had sat at the front of the stand and managed to step off before the collapse.

"This year, keep that arty crowd at the back," the Taoiseach ordered, "well out of sight." The Nod nodded and smirked to himself. He had arranged the collapse. It was part of his "Put 'im under pressure" policy. Mess things up and it was only a matter of time until the Taoiseach would crack. He would step into his shoes and get his job and of course the coat that went with it. He studied the coat hanging on a coat-stand close by.

"That's the coat for a real Taoiseach," he thought. "The lovely stitching and the cute velvet collar."

He stretched out his hand as if to touch it.

"Leave that coat alone," barked the Taoiseach, "and get back to work." The Nod looked away and scowled.

"Take your beady eye off that coat," the Taoiseach ordered. "People wouldn't recognise me in anything else. You stick to your anorak."

"Yes, Taoiseach," The Nod muttered and put his head down.

It was true that the Taoiseach wouldn't be recognised in anything else. The coat appeared in all the newspaper photographs. It was worn at every public function, arriving at airports, opening factories and meeting foreign visitors.

The Taoiseach picked up a letter from his desk and shook it at The Nod.

"Now, this letter from that silly woman. I want you to write to her and tell her once and for all that I will not put her name forward for the presidency," he snorted. "Just because she has run every two-bit committee from here to Timbuktu she thinks she would be the obvious choice." He glared at The Nod and continued on, "I never heard of The Brave Widows or The Ancient Monuments Society, but she writes to me every week. She also makes suggestions as to how I should run the country properly! She tells me that with her as President and me as Taoiseach we could establish a 'golden rule'."

He crumpled the letter in his fist.

"This is all your fault, Nod. You and your letter writing. I get two thousand letters a day, and most of them from cranks and film companies."

The Nod gloated inwardly as the Taoiseach fumed. As part of his "Put 'im under pressure" policy, he had convinced the Taoiseach that he could become even more popular if he got the public to write to him. And write to him they did, in their thousands. It seemed to him that every schoolchild, their mothers, fathers, aunts and uncles had taken pen in hand and written. Thousands of letters poured in every day. The Nod had insisted that each one should be personally answered. They worked late each night and never seemed to make inroads through the stacks of ever-growing letters. The Nod knew that the Taoiseach must crack soon. He glanced at the coat and smiled.

The telephone rang again.

"Don't dare answer it," the Taoiseach roared as The Nod whispered, "Hello" into the mouthpiece. "I won't speak to that crazy woman." The Taoiseach looked demented. The Nod's plan was working.

"It's another famous Hollywood film producer," The Nod whispered. "They want to speak to you."

"Tell them I'm out, gone away," the Taoiseach almost screamed. "I know what they want. They want to make a film here at government buildings. I overheard your telephone conversations. This is your doing, Nod. These people are everywhere." The Taoiseach sank into his chair, head in hands.

The Nod looked away and smiled to himself. He had encouraged the Taoiseach to build studios all over the country. It had been very successful and these days they were making films everywhere. Unfortunately, with so many film companies working in the country it was difficult to provide locations for them all. All the large public and state-owned buildings were being used. The Nod badly needed to find a large building for a remake of *Gone with the Wind*. Earlier that day, as he panted up the flight of stairs on his way to the Taoiseach's office, it occurred to him that their own building would be an ideal "Tara", if only he could convince the Taoiseach. Yes, already he could see Scarlet O'Hara dismounting from her horse and running up the front steps of their building. He had given the Taoiseach's direct telephone number to all the film directors.

It was almost as if the Taoiseach had read his thoughts.

"They can't have this building and that's that!" he thundered. When The Nod didn't reply at once the Taoiseach glared at him and sensed that something was afoot. He detected a shifty look in his eye.

"Don't even think about it, Nod," he hissed. "These film companies are everywhere. At a state dinner in Dublin Castle last week a crowd burst in wanting to see the film set of *Dracula*.

A woman came up to the Dutch ambassador who was eating his soup and told him he was 'the real thing, fangs and all.' It's just as well he didn't understand what she was saying. This sort of happening could cause the collapse of Europe, Nod."

"Yes, Taoiseach," The Nod replied, still thinking of Scarlet O'Hara running up the steps.

"Keep away from film directors and arty types," the Taoiseach ordered.

The Nod nodded, put the phone down and cut off the film director.

"And another thing," the Taoiseach continued, "since you are responsible for most of these letters from cranks and film directors, I expect you to stay behind each evening until they are all answered."

"But, Taoiseach, I have urgent business tomorrow evening," The Nod groaned, hoping to meet with the film director who had just phoned. If he could set them up with a location for "Tara" he might even get a part in the film.

"It's an order," the Taoiseach barked. "The first thing you'll do is write a strongly worded letter to the silly woman who wants to be President and finally warn her off. Cancel everything else!"

The Nod sighed, seeing his chance of stardom slip away. However, maybe it wasn't that bad, he might get locked in with the Taoiseach's coat and get the chance to practise wearing it. His heart skipped a beat as he glanced longingly towards the coat-stand.

The telephone rang again.

CHAPTER TWO

A Stranger in Torn Tights

From where they sat on the top of the hill they could almost see the whole of the county stretching beneath them. The spire of the church of the nearby market town was clearly visible among the patchwork of green fields. In the far distance the hazy outline of the Mourne Mountains sat on the skyline. Frank and Joan Kett were having a picnic. Rex, their dog, couldn't decide if he should watch them eating or study a clump of trees at the foot of the hill. He had seen a movement in the undergrowth at the edge of a small wood. If it proved to be a rabbit, a good chase would be better than a banana sandwich. The children munched and watched the clouds move across the sky.

"Two days here and it seems like two months," Joan sighed.

"It's better than school," said Frank.

"That's not the point," said Joan sharply. "We're on holidays anyway!"

"Well, I'm sure it's better than something..." he added, quite unconcerned. Rex was also unconcerned, lost in his thoughts as he waited for a rabbit to show.

He stretched out and studied his front paws.

"I'm a rabbit dog today," he thought. "If I was at home, chasing cats, I might be a cat dog."

He knew that there were all sorts of dogs. He'd heard the children talking about them: watch dogs, gun dogs, patrol dogs, blind dogs and even water dogs. He had never seen a water dog and wondered what it might look like. He imagined that it would carry water flasks around its neck and rescue thirsting souls lost in the desert.

"How heroic," he sighed as he watched the wind stir the tops of the trees below. Joan threw Rex a banana sandwich. He chose to ignore it and watch the trees again.

"I'd rather be back in the town with James and Dad than out in the country, wallpapering with Mum," Joan sighed. "Mum says James always falls on his feet," she added.

"So does a cat," said Frank.

"That's not what I mean," said Joan, impatiently. "Just because he's our older brother, he gets to stay at home and help Dad, while we're stuck out here mixing wallpaper paste for Mum."

"I wish there was a shop," said Frank. His pocket money was burning a hole in his pocket.

"I wouldn't mind if she could wallpaper, but most of the time it falls back on her face," Joan said.

"If I had my bike I could cycle to the town," Frank sighed.

"Auntie Joan only asked her to open the windows to air the place. I don't know why she decided to paint and paper the house. It must be guilt over something. I read in one of her magazines that people do strange things out of a sense of guilt."

They were staying with their mother in their aunt's house in Hacklim. Years ago their mother had promised their aunt that she would look after the house while she was abroad. An unexpected return had sent Mary Kett into a frenzy of decoration.

"It would be more fun working with Dad and James on the float for the parade," said Frank, "than stuck here in Hackim."

"Hack-lim," corrected Joan. "We're sitting on the Heights of Hacklim," she said, smoothing her dress. A movement at the bottom of the hill caught her eye. She saw a figure emerge from the trees and search for something in the undergrowth. Rex growled.

"Quiet, Rex," she whispered. The newcomer was a thin, weirdly-dressed elderly man.

"Strange," she thought.

From where she sat she was sure he was wearing tights or perhaps leggings. He was also barefoot. On his head he wore a flat black cap with a feather. His coat was short and trimmed with a fur collar.

The stranger hadn't seen the children yet and was gathering something in the grass.

'"That weirdo is eating nettles," Joan said with alarm.

"Won't they sting his mouth?" Frank asked.

"No, they're probably pet nettles – that type don't sting."

"He sure must be hungry. I'll give him a banana sandwich," said Frank and before Joan could stop him he was off down the hill with Rex at his heels.

The strangely dressed man heard them approach. He rose slowly and turned. He stared hard at Frank and asked, "Is it the time?"

Frank looked blank. "Time for what?"

Then the man looked blank.

"Goodness, I can't remember," he said. He looked puzzled.

"I think he wants to know the time," Frank said to Joan.

"Is it the time?" the man asked again.

The children looked at each other and shrugged. When they didn't answer the man looked disappointed, sighed and then began to study the ground again. Joan decided that she didn't like the look of this man. He looked as if he had slept in his clothes – for years. There was a fusty, damp smell. She decided that they should leave at once.

"Must hurry," she said. However, Frank thought that the man looked interesting and that they should stay for a chat.

"Have a sandwich," he offered. "Banana, they're good."

The strange man looked at the sandwich as if he had never seen one before, broke a piece off and chewed it slowly.

"A tasty sweetmeat," he said and smiled.

"Banana," Frank said. He had made a new friend.

Joan wasn't impressed.

"Mum will be expecting us home for tea," she said.

"But we've just had our tea," Frank protested. "She wants us to stay out of the way so that she can finish wallpapering."

" I will go too... if it is not time and nobody has been looking for me," the strange man said.

Frank looked disappointed.

"It's something to do with... horses," the man suddenly said. He looked as if he was trying hard to remember.

He smiled, shrugged his shoulders, then waved and disappeared back into the wood.

"I don't know why we have to go too," whined Frank.

"You can't be too careful these days," said Joan. "He could have been a pickpocket or worse. Anyway, he's gone."

Alarmed at the mention of a pickpocket, Frank at once checked his pocket money. When he found that it was all there he said, "Well I'm not going home yet. There'll be sticky old wallpaper all over the house."

"I know what we'll do," said Joan in her best bossy voice. "We'll visit the Jumping Church."

They made their way down the hill and joined the leafy laneway that led to the old churchyard. A man was working among the headstones.

"Look there's 'Fingers' Murphy," said Joan.

"Why is he called 'Fingers'?" asked Frank.

"Watch," Joan replied.

Unseen, they observed Fingers from behind the low stone wall that enclosed the churchyard. He was busy trimming a round green bush that stood among the lichen-covered gravestones.

"He's only using one hand," gasped Frank. He held the hedge clippers in one hand and clipped furiously. Bits of the bush flew everywhere. His other hand was tucked inside his jacket.

"They say there's something wrong with one of his hands," said Joan. "He never takes it out of his coat," she whispered. "It doesn't bother him as he can do as much with one hand as anybody else could with two." She was right. As they watched they saw him shape the hedge using his good hand to work the clippers. He worked quickly and as soon as he finished trimming he lifted a rake and gathered up the clippings in an instant.

Frank was amazed at his skill. "So, he's called Fingers because he's so good with them," he said.

"I suppose so," said Joan, not really sure.

They crossed the wall and moved towards the gate leading to the road. Fingers spotted them, dropped his rake and strode across the grass towards them to block their way. Up close, Joan thought he looked wild and menacing. She was having a bad day with strangers and wished they hadn't come this way. She gripped Frank's hand tightly.

Fingers smiled and she could see the gaps between his teeth.

"So you've come to visit the Jumping Church," he said.

CHAPTER THREE

Plans and Plots

Granny had telephoned Mrs Strong right away when she received the letter from The Nod, the Taoiseach's secretary. She was furious and paced up and down until her friend arrived.

Granny and Mrs Strong went back a long way. Old friends, they had been in many groups and organisations together. They had run the Brave Widows' Society for many years until they had been pushed aside by a group of younger and more ambitious widows. In recent years they had taken control of the Ancient Monuments Society, which they ruled with an iron fist allowing nobody to threaten their position.

The Ancient Monuments Society were building a float to enter for the National Parade. Granny's son-in-law, John Kett, and her grandson James were doing most of the work. Granny, who suspected deep down that John Kett must be good for something, had pressured him into planning and building the float. To her surprise, he had entered into the undertaking with great willingness and had been very clever.

They had borrowed an old open-decked bus from a friend in the motor business and John Kett had decided that it should be made to look like a castle on wheels. This involved cutting battlement shapes from plywood and fixing them to the upper part of the bus. Some unkind members of the Society were overheard to say that a bus with battlements was well suited to the "old battle-axe, herself". However, Granny thought that this was a marvellous idea for an Ancient Monuments Society. Work was progressing very well and it would be ready in time for the National Parade. At the moment, however, the float was the last thing on her mind. The Taoiseach's letter was of greater concern. The doorbell rang announcing the arrival of Mrs Strong. Granny let her in and with dignified silence led her to the living-room where she pointed to a chair at the table under the window. They sat opposite each other.

"He has refused the chance of a lifetime," she declared, barely able to control her anger.

"Who?" asked Mrs Strong.

"The Taoiseach, of course," snapped Granny. "We could have made a wonderful pair, him as Taoiseach and me as President," she added.

"As President?" Mrs Strong repeated, somewhat at sea.

"Don't you remember anything, Strong?" quizzed Granny. "I wrote to the Taoiseach and suggested that he should nominate me for President. With my experience of life and running committees, I would do a wonderful job. It's time they had another woman in that position. There's always someone to do things even better."

"Oh!" Mrs Strong replied and nodded, not wishing to disagree.

"Together, we could have had a 'golden rule'," Granny said wistfully and then more forcefully, "But it's too late now."

Mrs Strong didn't like the look in Granny's eye. It suggested that the matter wasn't over and done with yet.

The doorbell rang. It was John Kett and James. The bus for the parade was almost finished but John Kett had another idea he wanted to discuss. Granny, her thoughts elsewhere, reluctantly asked him in. He nodded to Mrs Strong as he entered the living-room. James sat quietly in the corner. His dad was obviously excited by his new idea.

"We must build a mangonel," he announced, "to tow along behind."

"A mangonel," Granny repeated looking at Mrs Strong. The blank look on her face made it clear that Mrs Strong didn't know what he was talking about either. However, Granny didn't want to let on that she didn't understand.

"It sounds like it could be a very good idea," she chanced. "And you would tow it along behind?" she asked.

"Yes, and we could use it to pretend we're attacking the castle, that is the bus of course," he laughed.

"Of course," Granny smiled.

"And we would fill the cradle with sweets and shower the crowd instead," John Kett said gleefully.

"A great idea to shower the crowd with sweets. Don't you think, Strong?"

Mrs Strong nodded in agreement, hoping she wouldn't be asked any further questions.

John Kett looked at his watch. "I must rush," he said, "I have to collect timber before the merchants close."

He turned to James, "I'll collect you later, when I off-load the trailer," he said.

"I'll go upstairs and read," James said. The bookshelves on Granny's landing were always worth a visit. Anyhow, Mrs Strong and Granny looked as if they didn't really want to be disturbed. They would be glad to see him leave the room.

They heard John Kett pull away outside and James went to go upstairs.

"A moment, James," Granny said. "Do you think your father is right about towing that thing behind?"

"The mangonel?"

"Yes, that."

James knew that Granny didn't know what they had been talking about. He thought he should explain.

"It's a machine that was used to attack castles. It's like a big spoon that throws rocks through the air. Dad thinks it would look great, being pulled behind the bus. It's the sort of thing they used hundreds of years ago to capture castles and then murder and kidnap people."

"Kidnap people," he heard Granny say. "Now that's an idea! There are always those who might well deserve to be kidnapped. In fact, a little kidnapping might do them a power of good." She turned to Mrs Strong and nodded thoughtfully.

James left and went upstairs. He didn't much like the look of Granny. He hoped that she wasn't going to get another of her strange ideas.

CHAPTER FOUR

Tales, Wails, Moans and Bones

Joan wished she had never heard of the Jumping Church. Fingers Murphy, as well as being the caretaker of the old cemetery, was also the local expert on the church ruins. He insisted that Joan and Frank should come and look at them. He ran a little ahead of them and called them forward with his good hand. The other he kept firmly tucked into his jacket.

"Look how the gable wall has jumped off its foundation!" he laughed.

He showed them the gable wall of the old church which stood upright a short distance away from its own foundation.

"What's a foundation?" asked Frank.

"It's the base on which they build walls," said Fingers.

"The wall is supposed to have moved when they buried the wrong person inside the church. It jumped to leave the grave outside the walls." Frank looked hard at the wall not quite sure what Fingers was talking about.

"Is that true?" asked Joan, having forgotten her fear of Fingers for the moment.

"Some say that a strong wind lifted the wall and dropped it there," said Fingers with a grin. "Who knows? There are many stories about this place," he added, glancing around.

Joan was all ears and Fingers could see that he had also caught Frank's interest.

"Tell us one," said Frank, now sitting on the edge of the wall.

"Well," said Fingers, "there's the story about the hill over there, where you've just had your picnic."

"You saw us then?" said Joan.

"You were sitting on the top of the Hill of Hacklim," he answered. "Close by is the fort of Garrett Iarla and there is an old story told around here that Garrett Fitzgerald, the Great Earl of Kildare, and his company of soldiers, together with all his court, sleep inside the hill."

"The hill we were sitting on?" asked Joan with a shudder.

"The very place," said Fingers. "It is said that they lie in an enchanted sleep, some even on their horses' backs, waiting for a six-fingered man to enter the cave and move the sword which hangs near the door. Then the spell will be broken, the warriors will awaken and they will ride out."

"There are soldiers inside the hill!" said Frank, his eyes as round as saucers.

"The story is that they will appear whenever the country needs their help," said Fingers.

"Have you ever seen them?" whispered Frank.

"No," said Fingers sadly, "but once, long ago, a man is said to have found his way into the cave and touched the hanging sword. The sleeping horsemen raised their heads slowly from their horses' manes. In fright, the man let the sword go. The warriors' heads dropped again and they have never since awakened."

"Is that true?" asked Joan again. "Has anybody ever seen Garrett Iarla?"

"Yes, they say that he alone of all his court can leave the cave. I heard a story of a man who was going to a fair to sell a horse and he was met on the road by Garrett Iarla, who offered to buy the horse. He sold it to Garrett who brought it into the cave. They say that Garrett's always short of horses."

"So he must come out of the cave from time to time," said Joan.

"Oh yes," said Fingers. "Some say that he makes his way out through an old dried-up well called Garrett's Well, up near the top of the hill."

"What makes him come out?" asked Frank.

"To look for horses, or perhaps it might be noise," said Fingers. "I heard that once it happened that there was a football match near the place and Garrett was awakened by the shouts. He came out and asked, 'Is it the time?' and was disappointed when no one could answer. He went back into the cave."

"What did he ask?" said Frank suddenly.

" 'Is it the time?' " replied Fingers.

Frank froze and looked at Joan who had turned pale.

"Oh no!" wailed Joan. "I think we've met him!"

"Nonsense, it's only a story," laughed Fingers. "He doesn't really exist."

"He does, he does!" cried Frank. "Oh, Joan, I feel sort of funny now." He was excited to think that he had shared his sandwich with a ghost or some such thing. Rex began to bark at the sound of raised voices. Joan didn't like any of this at all.

"Let's get out of here before it gets dark."

"But it's only early afternoon," said Fingers, puzzled at the change in the children.

"We've got to get home to help Mum with the wallpapering," lied Joan, pushing her way past Fingers. Frank followed shouting, "But I hate wallpapering... sticky, sticky mess."

He really wanted to stay and talk about Garrett, but he joined Joan on the road outside the churchyard.

"Anything is better than being haunted by an old earl who should have stayed dead," said Joan glancing around.

"And this is a very scary old graveyard," she added with a shudder.

"Look, Rex has a bone in his mouth," said Frank suddenly.

"Make him put it back," ordered Joan. "Whoever it belongs to will haunt us as well. Two ghosts in one day is more than enough. I've read stories about what happens to people who take bones home!"

Frank grinned and said in a deep voice, "Gimme back my bone!"

"Keep quiet, Frank, mocking is catching."

Rex, sensing that they were talking about his bone, ran off down the road ahead of them. Joan chased ahead and Frank followed behind shouting, "Gimme back my bone, Joan."

He would stop from time to time and double over laughing. When he reached the house Joan had locked the door and wouldn't open it until he said "Please, Joan" twenty times and admitted he was a dipstick. When, at last, she opened the door he pushed past her, but before he disappeared into the kitchen he whispered,

"Gimme back my bone, Joan."

He slammed the door and she could hear him chuckling to himself inside.

CHAPTER FIVE

The Plot Thickens...

James was familiar with Granny's collection of books and normally found them interesting. However, today it was difficult to settle down to read. Even Granny's collector's copy of Hitler's *Mein Kampf* didn't quite hold his attention and after ten minutes he got bored. On his way downstairs he stopped to study the pictures hanging along the wall. From there he could hear Granny and Mrs Strong in a heated discussion. James had always had a great interest in adults' conversation and loved to listen in at every chance.

"Little rabbit's have big ears," his mother would always say.

He sat on the bottom step outside the living-room door which was slightly ajar. If he listened hard he could almost hear everything they were saying. To his surprise they were talking about... the Taoiseach! Granny wasn't too pleased with him over something.

"He deserves to be taught a lesson," he heard her say.

Mrs Strong wasn't quite in agreement and said something about sending him another letter.

"I'm finished writing letters!" he heard Granny

shout. "It's time for proper action."

"What do you mean... action?" asked Mrs Strong.

"James gave me an idea," said Granny. Nobody was more surprised than James to find that he was part of all this.

"When he talked about kidnapping people, I decided that we should kidnap the Taoiseach!" said Granny.

"We?" said a shocked Mrs Strong.

"Yes, you and I. We can do it. It's simple really."

Mrs Strong must have looked very shocked as Granny tried to persuade her.

"The plan is simple. We disguise ourselves, hide somewhere in his offices and kidnap him some night when he works late. We'll only keep him overnight in a bed and breakfast somewhere and then let him go. We'll make it appear as if we rescued him and he'll be so thankful that he'll ask me to be President. He'll probably make you a senator or a minister or something."

The thought of being made a minister appealed to Mrs Strong.

"Perhaps the Minister for Minding Monuments," she beamed. "And I'd get a chauffeur-driven car with that job."

"Of course," said Granny encouraging her, "and a big fat pension."

Mrs Strong could see herself being driven in a big black limousine to the monthly meetings of the Ancient Monuments Society. Wouldn't the rest of the members be mad jealous?

"When do we do it?" she asked with enthusiasm.

"We have much to plan," said Granny. "I thought we might be able to arrange it around the time of the National Parade. The open-topped bus might even come in handy for making an escape!"

James was horrified. He couldn't believe his ears. Granny and Mrs Strong were going to kidnap the Taoiseach! To make matters worse, he had actually given her the idea. It was a madcap notion and with Granny at the helm it would either succeed or turn out to be a disaster. Heaven knows what might accidentally happen to the Taoiseach in Granny's hands. With him kidnapped, the country would be without a leader and in real danger.

"This is terrible," he said to himself. He could feel sweat on his forehead. "I'll have to do something to stop this."

He mustn't let Granny know that he knew everything. He quietly made his way back upstairs and waited on the landing. He could hear Granny and Mrs Strong moving about downstairs and eventually heard the front door slam and the sound of a car starting up. Mrs Strong had left.

He thought his dad would never come. At last he heard the doorbell and went downstairs to meet him.

Granny welcomed John Kett in. She had many questions about the float.

"When does the parade start?"

"All the floats line up at seven o'clock in the morning," John Kett answered.

"Perfect!" she muttered to herself and James could see that this fitted in with her plan.

"I may not travel with the bus that morning. Myself and Mrs Strong may be delayed and will join you later," Granny said.

James knew there was very little time.

Afterwards in the car he turned to his dad.

"Dad, Granny is going to kidnap the Taoiseach."

"No, not this year," his father answered. "It's a medieval theme this year. You know, the bus, the battlements, costumes and stuff. That must be next year."

James tried again, "Mrs Strong and Granny plan to kidnap the Taoiseach. That's very serious, Dad. I overheard them talking about it."

"You mean they intend to see the Taoiseach at the parade," he answered. "What person in their right mind would want to kidnap the Taoiseach, especially two elderly ladies like your Granny and Mrs Strong!" his dad laughed. "Don't start imagining things. You've been working too hard on the float, James."

The more James tried to argue the less his father appeared to listen. He was very worried, especially as he half blamed himself for giving Granny the idea to kidnap the Taoiseach.

He couldn't go to the police with his story as it was unlikely that they would believe him. He also thought of the shame of having his grandmother arrested. He imagined that he might have to identify her and Mrs Strong in a line up of criminal types. How would he ever explain to his mother that he had shopped his granny? Short of kidnapping his granny himself, things were looking pretty desperate.

CHAPTER SIX

Paste and Papering

Joan heard movement in the sitting-room and burst through the door protesting, "Mum it isn't fair the way that prat of a brother mocks me..." She stopped short and froze. A white shape stood in the centre of the room. It dripped a colourless liquid into a pool on the floor.

"Aghh!" she screamed. It had come to collect its bone. That damn dog was to blame. It was horrible, all sticky and messy. She knew the mess was called "plasma" and that ghosts and spirits leaked it. She was about to bolt for the door when the "spirit" actually spoke, "Joan, what's the matter with you?" it asked. To her further horror, it was using her mother's voice!

"What have done with my mother?" she heard herself scream.

"I am your mother," it answered, "under all this wallpaper and paste." Two hands appeared and lifted a fold of what she now recognised as wallpaper to reveal her mother's sticky face. "It's this damn wallpaper, it won't stay up and keeps falling back over my head. It has my hair and clothes destroyed."

"Oh Mum, you gave me a dreadful fright. For a minute I thought you were a ghost."

"I feel like one," Mary Kett said. "I can't get the hang of this wallpapering at all." Then she began to chuckle. "The hang of it... Get it?" she laughed and slapped her thigh. She slumped back in an armchair.

Joan began to laugh too. "Imagine me thinking you were a ghost. My mind is playing tricks on me. Ever since that dog ran off with the bone at the graveyard."

They giggled together for a while and then Mrs Kett said, "Joan, make me a cup of tea like a good girl. I'm parched with all this wallpapering." As she spoke another strip of wallpaper peeled off the wall and slipped to the floor in a sticky pile. She looked at it and then at Joan. She burst out laughing again. Joan left and went into the kitchen.

There was no sign of her smarmy brother anywhere. "He's probably stuffed his pesky face and gone to his bedroom," she said to herself.

She filled the kettle and switched it on. She stood, hand on hip, watching and waiting for it to boil. It had got dark early and she thought it must be coming on to rain.

The kettle was taking ages to boil. Suddenly, she heard a noise outside. She was sure it was that idiot brother lurking outside to try and frighten her or perhaps it was the dog coming back. She hoped he had got rid of the bone and shuddered at the thought. The noise of a bucket being knocked over outside made her glance towards the window.

"Aaagh!" she screamed as she saw the face looking in.

Garrett Iarla was tapping the window pane.

At the sound of the scream, her mother and Frank came running in.

"What's the matter, Joan? I heard you scream!"

"Oh Mum, it's him again," said Joan. "He's a ghost and I bet he thinks we have his bone."

"Nonsense, there's no such thing as ghosts." Her mother peered back at the face in the window. His clothes were certainly strange. She thought his little hat with the feather looked odd, but arty. It crossed her mind that arty folk might be good at wallpapering.

"He's our friend from the hill," said Frank, "I'll let him in." Before Joan could stop him he had unlatched the back door and Garrett sidled into the room.

"I can't find my way back," he said in a sheepish manner.

"Into the hill?" asked Frank.

"Yes," he replied. "I can't find the hole I climbed out of this morning."

"We can help you look for it," said Frank. "Rex will find it. We'll give him a bit of material for the scent."

"He doesn't need material for that. I can get it from here," said Joan twitching her nose.

"Joan," her mother cautioned.

"But Mum, he smells of old socks," whispered Joan.

"So would you if you were hundreds of years in a cave," muttered Frank under his breath.

Garrett didn't seem to hear or at least pretended that he hadn't heard.

"You must be hungry after all those years in the hill," said Frank. Garrett smiled and nodded. Frank turned to his mother, "Make him a sandwich, Mum, please!"

Mary Kett obliged while Joan glared at her. Rain lashed against the window and a sudden wind made the back door rattle.

"We're in for a bad night," said Mary Kett as she handed Garrett a sandwich. He munched it as if he hadn't eaten in years.

"It's too late for him to make his way back tonight," said Frank. "Can he stay please, Mum?"

"Well, I don't know," said Mrs Kett. "Won't someone be expecting you back at... the hill?" she asked hopefully.

"They're all asleep," Garrett said, licking his fingers.

"More sandwiches, Mum," whispered Frank.

Having used up all the bread for sandwiches, Garrett then

devoured the remainder of the contents from the fridge.

"There'll be nothing left for breakfast! " Joan protested. Her mother smiled at Garrett, hoping he hadn't heard.

"Can he stay, Mum?" Frank asked again. "We can't let him wander around outside in the dark."

"Oh, can't we?" Joan whispered.

"No, we can't, Joan," her mother said. "I'll finish wallpapering the room and he can sleep on the old sofa."

"Great," said Frank. "He and I can help you with the wallpapering. Can't we, Garrett?"

Garrett nodded, not quite sure what he was to help with.

However, after a slow start he proved to be a dab hand at hanging wallpaper. The room was finished in a very short time. Mary Kett was delighted and even Joan had to admit that it was fortunate that he stayed.

Later on when Garretts' snores filled the house, Frank wondered how he could have been so tired, having already slept in his cave for hundreds of years.

"It must be the wallpapering," he said to himself.

Thinking of the next day he tingled with excitement as he snuggled under his blankets. He was sure that he and Rex would find the way back into the cave. He couldn't wait to see inside.

Chapter Seven
Fears and Firkin

James could hardly open his eyes when his dad called him the next morning. He had tossed and turned worrying about Granny before he had finally fallen asleep. Over breakfast he tried to get his father to listen to him again.

"I tell you, Dad, it's serious," he said. "Granny and Mrs Strong intend to kidnap the Taoiseach."

His father hardly looked up from his breakfast. He was listening to the news on his walkman. James thought that this must be the worst of his dad's annoying habits. He was switched off when his radio was switched on. James kicked him on the shin. He looked up and passed the teapot.

"It might still be hot," he said, now intent on a notepad he was reading.

"The Taoiseach, not the teapot," James almost shouted.

"Of course," his dad said, "it says on the news that he'll be at the parade. You'll recognise him by his coat. He always wears the one with the velvet collar," he turned a few pages and then babbled on.

"I think that only those dressed as soldiers or crusaders should be on the top of the bus, to make it look like a castle." He switched off his radio. "We'd better hurry as there's a lot to do today. We have to check that the mangonet is finished... "

"Mangonel, not mangonet," James corrected, feeling a bit mean. He shouldn't have been too concerned as his dad wasn't listening. He was now engrossed in his notes.

"Miss Stitch wants to bring Firkin," his dad said.

"Firkin?" asked James.

"Her whippet," he said. "She's very attached to it and it goes everywhere with her," he added.

"That dog's a bag of nerves," said James. "It jumps at its own shadow. It can't travel on the bus. It'll end up doing something dreadful. I wouldn't be surprised if it jumps off the bus and bites the Taoiseach!"

His dad passed the teapot again.

"Well, I half promised her she could bring Firkin if she made up the costumes," he sighed. "And as she has them finished, it looks like Firkin is going to travel."

"Could mean trouble," said James moodily.

"Later this afternoon, we're going to Hacklim to collect your mother, Joan and Frank."

"Now about Granny, Dad!" James challenged.

"Goodness, look at the time. We must rush," said his dad, grabbing his notes and heading for the door.

James followed, muttering to himself.

They collected the mangonel from the workshop and towed it along behind the car. By the time they arrived at the bus quite a crowd had gathered. It was the final meeting of the members of the Ancient Monuments Society before the parade the next day. Bert, the bank manager, looked bothered. He had just received a telephone call from Granny that morning saying that she and Mrs Strong had been called away on important business and would not be at the meeting that day. They would stay overnight in the city and join the bus the following morning.

"I told you they're up to no good," said James. "I bet they're arranging the kidnap tonight."

"Your imagination is running away with you, James," his dad laughed.

"James thinks that Granny and Mrs Strong are going to kidnap the government," John Kett winked at Bert. They both laughed.

"The Taoiseach," James corrected. He could see that they were not taking him seriously and decided that he would say nothing further for the moment.

Miss Stitch tied Firkin to a lamppost and distributed the costumes. Soon an assorted collection of soldiers, crusaders, court ladies and milking maids gathered around the bus.

"Soldiers on the top of the bus and the maidens below," John Kett shouted, arranging the seating.

A murmur of protest arose from the ladies.

"Firkin can't travel downstairs. He must be in the open air," Miss Stitch shouted.

"I hope we're not taking 'Firkin the Frenzied' again this year," groaned Bert. "He went berserk on the last trip when he heard an ambulance siren and flooded the bus. All those sitting on the outside of the seats got wet legs."

Heads nodded in the background, mostly from those who had suffered. Miss Stitch was determined, "If Firkin doesn't travel then neither do I... and I want my costumes back." There was silence. Miss Stitch, sensing that her moment had come, quietly added, "Firkin deserves an apology." She lifted Firkin, glared at John Kett and stood waiting.

John Kett was in a muddle. If Firkin didn't travel then neither did Miss Stitch's costumes and the float would be a disaster. He looked pleadingly at Bert.

"Sorry, Firkin," Bert sheepishly muttered and walked away.

Miss Stitch smirked. She hadn't liked that bank manager since he had refused her a loan to buy a new sewing machine. It was good to get one up on him.

It took the rest of the morning to sort matters out. Finally it was agreed that both soldiers and maidens could sit where they liked on the bus. John Kett collected the family's costumes from Miss Stitch and agreed the starting-out time next morning.

By now James had given up trying to get through to his dad about Granny. He decided that his next target should be his mother. She might believe him. It was early afternoon when they finally set off for Hacklim. They took the bus so that they could get an early start the next morning. Normally it would have made a curious sight travelling through the countryside. Glancing up from their work, people thought that it was yet another prop being brought to the latest film location.

CHAPTER EIGHT

Garrett's Well

That morning Frank awoke at first light and set about getting the others up. Garrett and Joan jumped out of their beds but his mother refused to wake up. Later on, as they left through the back door, her snores resounded behind them. She was happily dreaming of beautiful wallpaper patterns.

Rex had been up even earlier checking out suspected rabbit holes in the neighbourhood. The last one he visited turned out to be occupied by a resentful badger who attacked before he could even introduce himself. His rear still hurt.

Garrett, who Joan thought was most forgetful, couldn't remember where he had emerged from the cave. They explored the hill on every side and found nothing that appeared like an opening.

Rex refused to sniff out any more burrows.

"I remember that when I crawled out there was a stone wall on each side," Garrett said, scratching his head.

They then examined all the stone walls around the hill and found nothing that Garrett recognised.

"Perhaps you just dreamed about the cave," said Joan, certain that this was a person who imagined things. It crossed her mind that he might be a lunatic who had escaped from somewhere. Wherever that was, he had been taught wallpapering. It was probably like sewing mailbags in prisons.

Garrett sat down on the grass and scratched his head again. He looked sad.

"We'll lift flat stones," said Frank trying to be helpful.

"The only thing you'll find under flat stones are insects... like yourself," said Joan.

"Cop on, Joan, there might be a stairs or ladder that would lead us to the cave."

"Hmm," said Joan. Garrett said nothing.

Rex suddenly howled and chased off across the hillside in hot pursuit of a rabbit. This was much more interesting that being forced to sniff old and dangerous burrows.

The rabbit disappeared into a thicket of thorn and briars. Rex followed.

"He'll be back in a moment," said Joan. "He's afraid of dark holes."

But he didn't come back. Five, ten, fifteen minutes passed and there was no sign of him.

"We'd better go and look," said Frank. "He's probably caught in a rabbit trap."

They walked around the thicket looking for the best way in.

Garrett perked up. "I ripped my hose on these thorns yesterday," he said, picking up a piece of cloth.

"I didn't see you with a hose," said Frank.

"Oh no, I wear the hose," he said, pointing to his tights.

"What next?" thought Joan, " ...wearing a hose indeed!"

Garrett held up the piece of cloth and said, "Look, I must have come this way." He made his way through the bushes and the children followed.

"This must be Garrett's Well," gasped Joan as she recognised the dried-up well that Fingers had spoken about. It was a stone-lined hole in the ground. "This must be the way in," Garrett announced.

"Don't you remember anything?" asked Joan as Garrett scratched his head yet again.

Frank peered into the hole and called, "Rex!"

There was no answer. "It looks very dark in there." He looked at Garrett.

"Should we go in and get Rex?" he asked. Garrett shrugged and looked away. He seemed afraid.

"It's your well!" said Joan, amazed.

"I don't like the dark," whispered Garrett.

"Well, I'll go in," said Joan firmly. She hesitated and then said, "As soon as I get a torch." She stamped off, leaving Garrett and Frank looking into the hole. Frank shouted into the well from time to time while Garrett sat on the grass and waited.

After a while they heard voices approaching and Joan appeared through the brambles followed by Fingers Murphy. He had brought a shovel and Joan was carrying a large torch.

"Fingers said he would help and he gave me his monster torch," Joan said. "I bet he's not afraid of the dark!" she added, glancing at Garrett who looked a little shame-faced.

Fingers shone the torch into the hole.

"Well, who's going in?" asked Joan. Nobody answered. Garrett turned away and whistled under his breath. Joan stared at Frank and his bottom lip began to quiver.

"'Then I'll do it myself,' said the Little Red Hen'!" As the others stood and watched, Joan picked up the flashlight and levered herself through the opening.

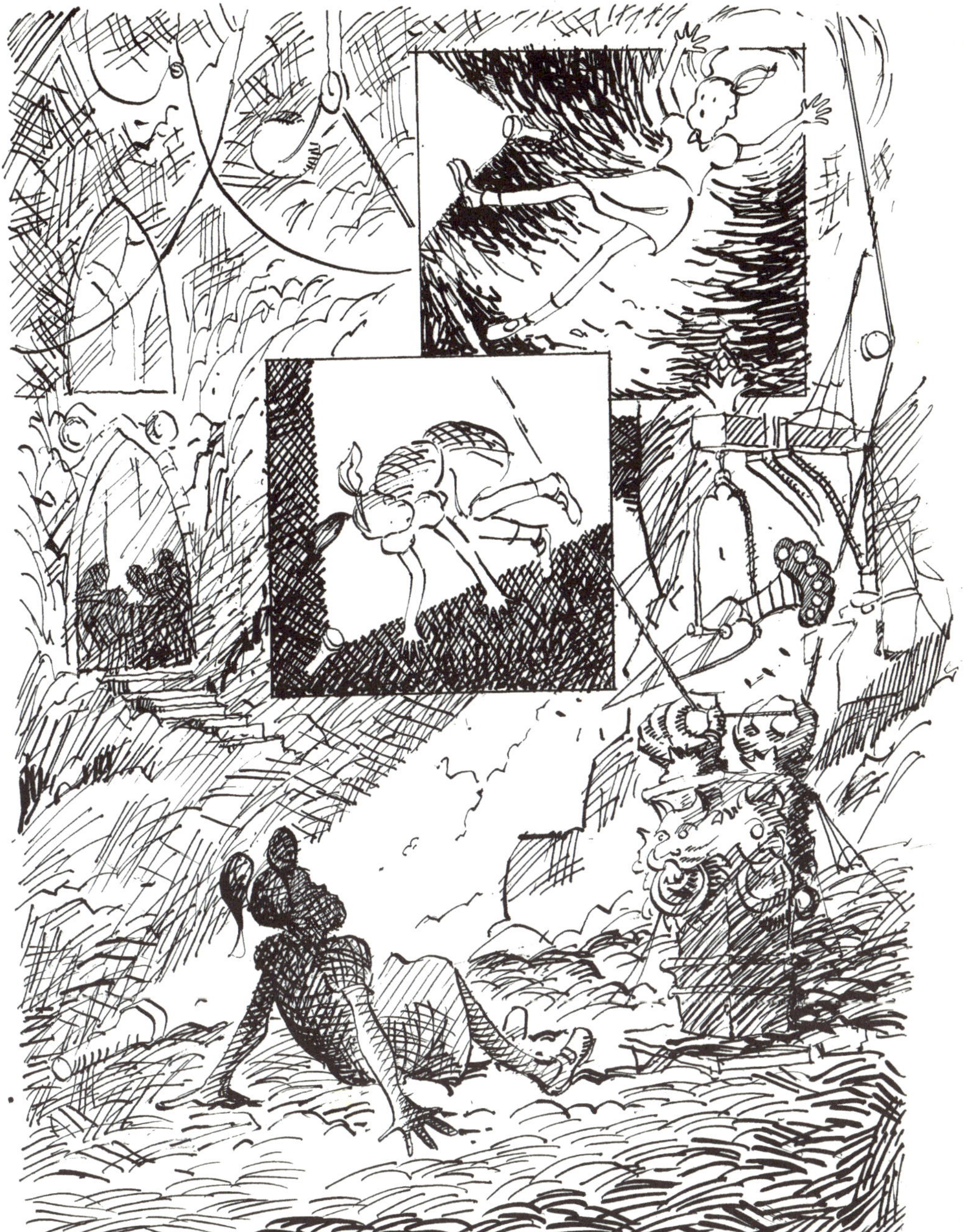

As she switched on the torch, the ground gave way and she slid downwards into the dark. Taken by surprise she dropped the flashlight as she tumbled to the bottom.

She landed in an underground chamber, dimly-lit by a shaft of daylight from the hole through which she had fallen. The fallen torch showed an enormous sword, hanging from the roof. As she looked upwards she could see that it was connected by ropes to all sorts of funny-looking gadgets. A light breeze caused the sword to sway. The wind made a low moaning sound. This was scary and Joan wasn't sure if she wanted to go any further. Then she heard another noise that made her blood chill. A low snoring sound came from somewhere deep inside the hill. That was enough. She scrambled back up the earthen slope quicker than she had slid down and burst back into the light. Frank, Garrett and Fingers were surprised at her sudden reappearance.

"There's nothing down there," she gasped, quite out of breath, "and there's certainly no sign of Rex."

"Nothing?" asked Frank with a disappointed voice.

"The poor little dog," said Fingers sadly.

"Not even a way into the cave?" asked Garrett in a downcast voice.

"Nothing much interesting anyway," Joan replied. Nobody was going to get her into that dark hole again.

"Rex will make his own way home and if not, we'll come back tomorrow and search again," she said.

Frank and Garrett looked miserable.

"Look," she said, "it's long past lunchtime and I'm starving. I'm off home."

She headed down the hill with the others following slowly.

CHAPTER NINE

Hide and Seek

Granny and Mrs Strong arrived outside government buildings and joined the small queue of people waiting for the conducted tour. Among the group were some Americans, a Japanese person and a distracted-looking father with a small boy. He had stopped the child drawing on the low stone wall outside the gate and confiscated his box of crayons. As Granny and Mrs Strong arrived the boy was throwing a tantrum and jumping up and down on his father's foot. Granny, who firmly believed that "children should be seen and not heard", thought this behaviour was terrible. As they waited in line she watched and suffered the child's antics.

When he kicked his father on the shins she decided that they had all had enough. She stretched out her umbrella, hooked the boy's collar from behind and yanked sharply. Taken by surprise the youngster was jerked backwards and fell on his bottom on the hard pavement. When he looked around Granny was busy talking with Mrs Strong.

"That should teach the horrid child a lesson," Granny whispered.

The "horrid child" eyed her with mistrust. The boy's father looked grateful. Happy that she had stopped the brat's tantrum, Granny plucked a list from her handbag and turned to Mrs Strong.

"Time to check, Strong."

"Certainly," was the reply. Mrs Strong peered into her carrier bag and said, "Torch, tea, uniforms and mobile phone all here."

"Excellent!" said Granny.

The guide opened the gate and admitted the waiting group. Their baggage was checked as they filed through. The security guard questioned Mrs Strong about the contents of her carrier bag. She explained that she was a nurse who could be called on duty at any moment. Hence the telephone and the flashlight. Granny smiled and nodded innocently. The security guard returned her smile and said, "Carry on."

The large water fountain burst into spray as they passed through the courtyard. Coins shimmered under the water. For luck, the Americans threw in a handful of loose change. The group entered the main building.

Granny and Mrs Strong had planned to find somewhere to hide within the building until after dark. Disguised as cleaning ladies they would sneak upstairs to his office and kidnap the Taoiseach. The press and the radio would be telephoned as soon as he was seized. They had already booked a bed and breakfast where they would hide until they decided it was safe to let him go...

The tour guide welcomed the visitors and hoped they would enjoy the tour.

"Unfortunately we will be unable to visit the Taoiseach's office today, as he is busy answering the many letters he has received from you, the public." Some of the group looked disappointed but not the small boy who was busy trying to pull the brass rails from the red carpet on the lobby stairs. He roared when his father clipped his ear and the group moved on to view the ceremonial staircase.

Granny and Mrs Strong hardly listened as the guide described the staircase. They had found a suitable hiding place. They hung back until the coast looked clear and then crawled into the dark space under the stairs.

"Perfect so far!" Granny announced.

"I've brought a flask," said Mrs Strong. "Time for tea."

They settled comfortably and Mrs Strong was pouring a second cup of tea, when a small cross face peeped around the corner and said, "What are you doing in there?"

It was the horrid child. The ladies were dumbfounded and, for a moment, at a loss for words.

"I'll tell on you," he said. "You shouldn't be in here."

Granny couldn't believe it. Was this infuriating pest about to blow their cover? She knew exactly what to do. With years of experience humouring children, she looked the child straight in the eye.

51

"How clever of you to find us!" she smiled, and nudged Mrs Strong, who then joined in. "We knew that you would find us and win the prize."

"The prize?" the child asked, his eyes widening.

"The first prize," nodded Mrs Strong.

"The hide and seek prize," said Granny. "I think you've won, but you mustn't tell anyone or they'll want it too."

"Where is it? Tell me or I'll scream. I'm very good at screaming," he added.

"I bet you are," Granny said to herself and forced a smile again. She thought very hard.

"The prize is in the fountain at the front of the building. It's full of money and you are allowed to take as much as you like."

The boy looked doubtful and eyed both of the ladies.

Mrs Strong spoke softly, "Think of all the sweets you could buy! Ice cream, toys and anything you might wish for."

The child looked longingly towards the courtyard. They knew they had him hooked.

"You mustn't tell anyone that you have won the prize because they will want it too, and unfortunately if anyone else finds us we have to tell them about it," Granny purred.

The horrid child disappeared at once and headed towards the fountain. They smiled as they saw him wade through the water spray. A security guard spotted him and shouted at him to come out.

"Get knotted," the child screamed and scurried back into the middle. Out of sight in the spray, and soaking wet, he worked hard, cramming his pockets full of coins. His father arrived and stared with disbelief at his son in the fountain.

"Come out at once," he roared and attempted to pull the boy from the pool.

"Get lost, Dad," the child screamed and refused to leave.

"Mind your language," his dad shouted and managed to

clip him on the ear.

They chased around the pool, father following son. Visitors and security guards gathered around, enjoying the show.

Granny and Mrs Strong were well pleased. They had managed to distract all attention from themselves and were delighted that the brat was now soaking wet and being chased around the fountain by his father.

In spite of them the little horror was enjoying himself. His pockets were bulging and he hadn't had such fun all day.

His father finally captured him and carried him off squirming. With all the excitement the two ladies hadn't been missed. They poured another cup of tea, smiled and settled back to wait.

CHAPTER TEN

The Cavern

Joan was halfway down the hill when she saw James and her dad approaching. She waved and ran towards them.

"Am I delighted to see you, Dad!" she said. "I've had a day of it. We've been trying to find the way into the cave to get your man back and then we lost Rex."

"Your man?" her dad asked.

"Garrett the Nutter," she replied, "who thinks he lives somewhere under the hill. Of course, Frank believes him," she added.

"Hold on," her dad said trying to get a grasp of what she was saying. His head was already in a spin listening to James talking about Granny. He hadn't stopped all day about a plot to kidnap the Taoiseach. Now, here was Joan talking about Garrett the Nutter, whoever he might be. It was at times like this that he really wondered about his family.

"Start again!" he said to Joan. He managed to slow her down and get her to tell him all that had happened during the past two days. She told him how they had found Garrett, who had wallpapered the house and then stayed overnight, and how they had set out that morning to find the cave. She explained that so far they had only succeeded in losing Rex.

"Where is Rex?" James asked.

"He followed a rabbit down Garrett's Well and I couldn't him find down there," Joan said.

"You went down the hole?" her dad asked.

"Oh, there was nothing down there, only the old sword hanging down from the roof."

"Only the old sword!" said a voice behind her. "You

never said anything about that." Fingers had arrived.

His eyes lit up as he shouted up the hill to Garrett and Frank.

"We've found the way in!"

Joan ignored him and turned to her father, "It's scary, Dad, I heard strange noises." Then she whispered, "Send Frank in first... it's his dog."

"It's our dog," said James crossly. "We'll all go in together."

Five minutes later they all stood looking down the hole deciding who should go first. It was agreed that the adults would lead and the children would follow.

Joan hadn't mentioned the sudden drop and the three grown-ups landed in a heap at the bottom. The children followed and all six ended in a jumble of arms and legs.

"Frank, take your foot out of my mouth," Joan roared, "I can taste your rotten old sock."

"It's not my foot," Frank shouted.

"I'm sorry, it's my elbow," said Garrett.

There was silence for a moment.

Joan now knew that not only did Garrett's clothes smell like old socks but they also tasted that way too.

She switched on the torch but couldn't see her dad in the tangle of bodies.

"Where are you, Dad?" she called.

"Here," a voice answered from somewhere underneath. He crawled out, stood up and checked himself.

"I think I'm fine," he said. "Goodness, my radio, I hope it's all right." He pulled the radio with dangling headphones from his pocket. He switched it on, checked it and then stuffed it back into his pocket.

"Now, what's this?" he said, looking at the sword hanging from the ceiling.

"It's the sword that opens the cave," said Fingers in a hushed voice. "Isn't that right, Garrett?"

Garrett looked blank. "I think so, but I can't remember for sure." he said, scratching his head.

"Definitely an escaped something… " Joan said to herself.

Her dad looked at the sword and studied the contraption from which it hung.

"If I pull the handle, the sword will spin," he announced smugly.

"Here goes," he said. He pulled and tugged but nothing happened. His face was red with the effort.

"Must be broken," he said. "Well that's that!" He looked at his watch. "Goodness, it's nearly time for the news." He searched in his pocket for his radio.

"Let Garrett try," said Frank, pulling him towards the sword.

Garrett wheezed with effort as he hung from the handle. Nothing happened. Frank looked disappointed and Joan smirked as if to say, "I told you so."

"I'll try," said Fingers. His eyes were bright and his face had a curious expression.

Joan was never sure what exactly happened next. He moved very quickly and in the dim light she thought that he pulled out the hand from inside his jacket. He grabbed and quickly tugged the handle. For a split second she thought she saw six fingers. In fright she let the flashlight drop and the chamber plunged into darkness. What happened next was terrifying. The gadgets and contraptions in the ceiling began to move. A strange whirring and clacking was heard in the darkness. "Switch back on the flashlight," someone yelled. Joan searched and found it on the floor. She attempted to switch it on.

"Dad, it doesn't work," she screamed in panic.

"Has anyone got a light?" her dad asked.

"I might have a flint," said Garrett. "If I can find some kindling."

"Some what?" shouted Frank.

A low snoring sound came from somewhere close by in the darkness.

Further away, a splintering and cracking sound was heard. Daylight began to slowly filter through a small doorway which they hadn't noticed in the dark. It led to a larger cavern which had begun to fill with light. The snoring came from this direction.

Curiosity overcame fear as they squeezed through the door and found themselves staring at an almost unbelievable sight. A large gap had opened in the side of the hill. The setting sun beamed through and flooded the inside of a large cave with a golden light. The roof of the cavern was propped up with stone columns and huge timber beams. The sunlight lit every nook and cranny and also the curious slumbering groups of people that lay around on the floor. Bookshelves, packed with scrolls, parchments and leather-bound volumes stood against the walls. The sun caught the gold leaf titles and made them glint. Heavy antique furniture lay scattered across the floor or stacked against the walls. Oak chests lay open, their contents of plates and clothes strewn around.

A large ornate chair stood on a raised platform in the centre of the cave. Frank recognised at once the small dog that looked up from the seat.

"It's Rex!" he shouted. Rex barked and jumped down.

The sleepers on the floor stirred.

"I remember now," smiled Garrett. "This is my court. I was

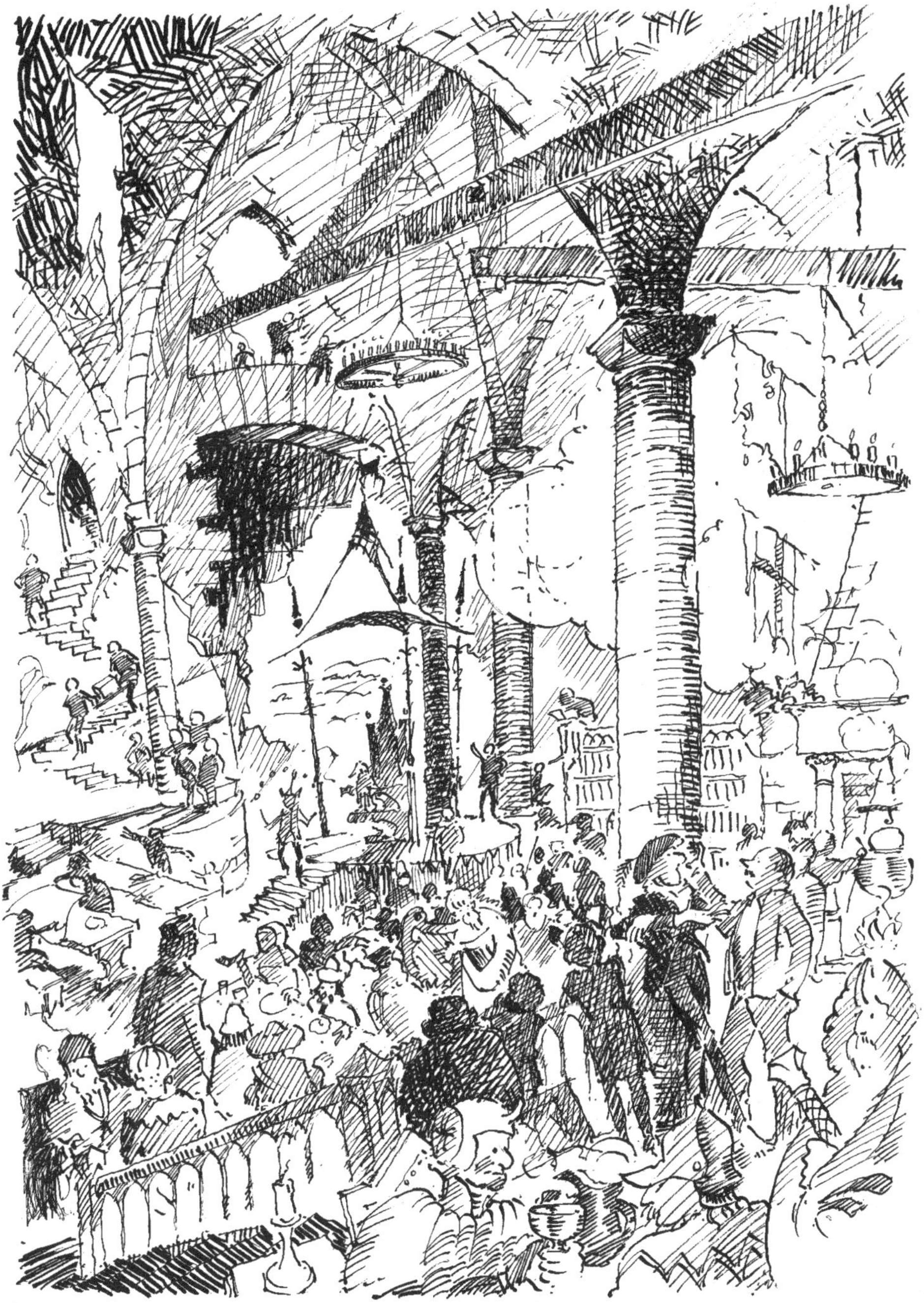

brought here from somewhere. They almost chopped off my head."

"Who brought you here?" asked John Kett.

"It's so long ago, it's difficult to remember. I was once king of this country in all but name," he sighed wistfully.

"King of this country?" asked James.

"It's all in the history books," said John Kett.

"The people of the mounds, or the *sidhe*, brought me here." said Garrett.

"For the birds," said Joan to Frank, nodding towards Garrett.

He strode across the floor, new life in his step. He stopped at the first group of sleepers, a fierce-looking group of warriors with helmets and long swords. They awoke at his touch, peered up and rubbed their eyes.

"These are my gallowglasses or soldiers."

"Aren't they supposed to be sitting around on horses?" asked Frank, a note of disappointment in his voice. "You said so, Fingers," he pouted.

"Horses are hard to get," said Garrett. "If you knew the trouble I've had to go to, to get the few we have." He pointed to three sorry-looking nags in the corner.

"Apart from the bother of finding them, can you imagine trying to drag them through that hole we came through? It's no joke."

"Didn't they supply you with horses when they brought you here?" asked James.

"No they didn't," said Garrett abruptly, losing his patience. "They must have forgotten about them. I'm sure they can't remember everything." That ended the conversation about horses, for the moment.

It seemed to Frank that if the legend was meant to have

people asleep on horses then it was a pity that they had to sit around on the floor in untidy groups.

"Maybe legends aren't all they're cracked up to be!" Garrett said crossing the floor.

The gallowglasses looked a trifle bad-tempered having being awakened suddenly after five hundred years.

Garrett moved on and gently touched the next group. As they awoke, he introduced them as a Brehon or judge, a doctor and a harper poet. The poet, a wild-looking character wrapped in a kind of blanket, leapt to his feet. He grabbed a large harp and burst into high-pitched chant.

Garrett winced, listened politely for a while and then interrupted.

"Thank you very much, Keenan. A marvellous praise song. I'd love to hear the rest later... much later."

Keenan looked disappointed having been cut off at the twentieth verse with only fifty more to go.

"What was that all about?" James asked his dad.

"The poets composed poems that told of brave exploits and that sort of thing. I believe it could often take days to recite one poem," whispered John Kett.

"Phew, it was a stroke of luck that Garrett stopped him," said James.

"Still, it might have been interesting," said John Kett.

"Dad, you haven't forgotten about Granny?"

"Shh, not now, not here, James," hushed his father.

The next group to awaken were the jesters and the gamblers. Then he woke the tailors and the other musicians. Soon the whole court with all its attendants were awake.

Keenan was annoyed that Garrett had woken the musicians. As they played on their lutes and pipes Keenan struck up a tune on his harp. The noise was terrible and soon everyone began to complain. The gallowglasses threw plates.

Everyone took to ducking. It looked as if it might get even more dangerous when an axe whizzed through the air in Keenan's direction. Suddenly, the whole place was in a terrible tumult.

"Quiet!" Garrett roared, and banged on a big drum.

The din ceased at once. Garrett looked annoyed as he sat back in the big chair and glowered. When the crowd had quietened, he began to speak. "You will really have to try to get on better, until such time as we are called to help the country."

"I hope it's not another five hundred years!" shouted a wag from the floor. Garrett ignored him.

A fierce-looking gallowglass stood up, a wild glint in his eye.

"How's about a cattle raid, to pass the time?" he roared, rubbing his hands.

The other gallowglasses became excited at the thought of a cattle raid. Garrett shook his head and the mumbling almost ceased.

"Spoilsport," the wag shouted from somewhere at the back.

"What's a cattle raid?" Frank asked his dad.

"The old Irish considered it a form of sport to steal their enemies' cattle," he answered.

"That's rustling," said Frank. "That could be fun!"

The cave was now a-buzz with activity. Tables were being set up, seats straightened and floors swept. A huge fire had been lit which crackled up the chimney. The sun had almost set and with the approach of darkness the flickering firelight danced merrily on the walls.

But the gallowglasses looked restless.

CHAPTER ELEVEN

Terrorist Tactics

Meanwhile, back at government buildings, the Taoiseach put down his pen. "Time for a break, Nod, I've just signed my fifteenth hundred letter and I've got writer's cramp." He flexed his arm to relieve the stiffness and looked up to catch The Nod staring at his coat again.

"Don't even think about it, Nod!" he said. Rubbing his eyes, he placed his glasses on his desk and got up to make a cup of tea. He went into the small kitchen beside the lift shaft and boiled the electric kettle. He opened the fridge to get the milk.

"Drat!" he swore on finding that there was none.

He would get The Nod to go to the corner shop to buy a carton. On second thoughts, he decided to go himself. A walk in the night air would do him good.

He didn't bother to tell The Nod that he was going out. He simply stepped into the lift and quickly dropped to street level.

The Nod looked up when he heard the hum of the lift. He checked the small kitchen and saw that the lift had gone down. Looking out the window, he saw the Taoiseach cross the road. He tingled with excitement. He had the office to himself for at least the next ten minutes. More importantly, he was alone in the office with the beautiful coat. He couldn't believe his luck. It was worth working late for such a reward. He checked the kitchen again to be double sure. His heart beating, he tip-toed towards the coat-stand. Lifting the coat carefully he caressed it lovingly and slipped it on. As he twirled, whirled and pirouetted across the floor, he said to himself, "Someday this will be mine, all mine."

The coat made him power-crazed. It was almost... as if he

was the Taoiseach. Puffing out his chest he spoke to his own empty chair,

"Do this, Nod," he gibbered. "Do that, Nod," he ordered. He punched the air with his finger. He fixed his hair and

imagined he looked like the Taoiseach. Striding across the room, he threw himself into the Taoiseach's chair. He found the Taoiseach's glasses and placed them on his nose. Opening the top drawer, he took out one of the Taoiseach's long black fat cigars. With his feet on the desk, he leaned back and lit it. He blew a large smoke ring and watched it float towards the ceiling. He could feel real power. He was the Taoiseach.

The door opened and two strange-looking cleaning ladies stood framed against the light from the corridor.

"Can't you even knock?" he scowled. He was angry at having been disturbed.

To his surprise, the intruders didn't reply.

"Come back later, can't you see the Taoiseach's busy?" he shouted, blowing another smoke ring.

The two ladies ignored the order and moved deftly towards him. Pulling a cloth sack from a carrier bag one of them held it out.

"OK then, OK, fill your rubbish sack and get out of here quickly!" he coughed.

He was amazed that they never answered him as they closed in. He placed the lit cigar in the ashtray on the desk and then looked up.

The taller lady stared him straight in the eye and before he could say another word she popped the sack over his head.

"Got ya," Granny shouted in delight.

"We've caught the big fish here," said Mrs Strong. "I'd recognise his coat anywhere."

"Easy peasy," said Granny as she spun him around and loosely tied his hands together behind his back.

The Nod spluttered under the sack, which was now pulled over his shoulders.

"Of course, you'd know the coat anywhere," said Granny brushing it off and pulling the squirming figure to his feet. The

Nod slobbered as he tried to explain that he wasn't the Taoiseach. He couldn't be heard under the sack.

The lift hummed and the indicator light glowed. It was on the way up.

"Someone's coming," hissed Mrs Strong, her eyes popping.

Granny ran over to the lift, fumbled around and opened the control panel door.

"I'll take care of this," she said. She fiddled with something and suddenly the indicator light went out.

"I've taken the fuse out," she said gleefully. "Whoever is in this lift is stuck," she laughed. "We have the place to ourselves." They whooped like naughty schoolgirls, enjoying themselves. The telephone rang on the Taoiseach's desk.

"Quick, let's get out of here," said Mrs Strong.

"Not so soon," said Granny, winking as she picked up the phone. Her eyes sparkled as she sat on the desk and leaned back, quite relaxed.

"Hello, the Taoiseach's office," she answered in her best posh voice.

She listened for a moment and then to Mrs Strong's horror she continued to speak.

"No, I'm sorry but you can't speak to the Taoiseach at present. He's a little unwell," she sniggered looking towards the struggling Nod.

"Who is speaking?" she asked. "The *National Press*," she repeated, "You wish to ask the Taoiseach who he will be sitting beside at the National Parade this year?" She smiled at Mrs Strong who with the crook of her umbrella, was leading the unfortunate Nod by the neck towards the door.

"The Taoiseach will be unavailable for a while. I'm sure he will give you an interview when he returns." She turned to Mrs Strong. "This is our chance to announce the kidnap. We have enough time to get away." Mrs Strong nodded as she pulled The Nod along.

"Hello," Granny spoke into the phone. "The Taoiseach has just been captured by the A.C.B." She listened as the reporter questioned her further.

"Yes, I suppose you could describe us as a new terrorist group," she answered.

"The A.C.B. are the Abandoned Cat's Brigade, and we mean business."

Mrs Strong doubled over laughing as Granny continued, "The Taoiseach will be returned when the ransom is paid... to the Abandoned Cats' Home." She slammed the phone down, clenched her fists and shouted, "The deed is done."

The Nod, bag on head and wearing the Taoiseach's coat, was bundled out the door and down the corridor. He hopped along, pushed and pulled by the ladies.

On reaching the top of the staircase, they saw two security guards running towards them. They had heard the disturbance and had come to investigate.

"Quick," Granny said, "take the other stairs." This was the ceremonial staircase, close by. As the guards rushed up one staircase they ran down the other. At the bottom, they found the doors to the courtyard locked with even more guards outside.

"We've got to hide until the coast is clear," Granny announced.

"Where?" asked Mrs Strong. She had The Nod in an arm lock and his muffled shouts could be heard echoing through the hallway. She whispered a death threat through the bag and his cries stopped immediately.

"Back under the stairs, until things settle," ordered Granny. The Nod was pushed forward into the darkness and Granny and Mrs Strong followed. All three crammed in together. They sat with their knees in their mouths listening to the guards running up and down the stairs overhead. Things were not going exactly to plan, but Granny was confident that she was in full control.

Meanwhile, the real Taoiseach, stuck in the lift, was furiously pressing buttons and shouting as loud as he could. Nationwide, a solemn-looking announcer appeared on television and informed the country that the Taoiseach had been kidnapped by rebel cat lovers. Cats' homes all over the country were about to be picketed.

Granny and Mrs Strong, with the unfortunate Nod, settled under the stairs for another wait.

Chapter Twelve
The Time, The Time...

In spite of the air of festivity within the cave the gallowglasses were unhappy and complained amongst themselves. They wanted a cattle raid. Garrett watched, worried that they might cause trouble. To distract them, he nodded to Keenan to strike up another tune on the harp. The poet gladly obliged but the gallowglasses, with a cattle raid on their mind, weren't quite in the humour for another praise song. After a few groans another axe was let fly.

"Duck, Dad!" roared James.

John Kett ducked, dodged and side-stepped. He stood on Rex, lost his balance and fell flat on his face. The gallowglasses, who found this hilarious, quite forgot about their cattle raid for the moment and burst out laughing. Garrett looked pleased with the distraction. Joan wasn't impressed.

"Don't be so embarrassing, Dad," she said. "Falling about in front of this smelly lot!"

Her dad picked himself up.

"Goodness, my radio," he said. "I hope it's all right." He pulled it out of his pocket and plugged in the earphones.

"It sounds OK," he said relieved. Suddenly he frowned, turned pale and looked at James.

"What's the matter, Dad," asked James.

"There's been a newsflash," his dad stammered. "The Taoiseach has been kidnapped. The whole country in on alert."

James' face turned as white as his dad's. He shook his head slowly.

"I bet it's Granny. I told you that this was going to happen."

Fingers and the children gathered around. They all looked very worried.

"What's the meaning of this?" asked Garrett.

"The Taoiseach, the leader of our country, has been kidnapped," said John Kett.

"And by our Granny," James added glumly.

"Will she kill him?" Garrett asked in amazement.

"Perhaps... but not intentionally," said James. "Anything might happen to him in Granny's hands. She's not a responsible type of person."

"Then if the leader of the country is kidnapped, there is nobody in charge!" said Garrett becoming suddenly excited.

"I suppose you could say that," said John Kett.

"Then the country is in danger!" said Garrett, his eyes ablaze. Without further ado, Garrett strode to the chair in the middle of the cave. He banged the big drum and called for silence. The cave went quiet.

"At last, it is the time," he roared. Cries of "The time, the time" resounded around the hall. Gallowglasses stood up and cheered. A ripple of excitement travelled around. "The country has need of us," Garrett roared. They were about to fulfil the legend. They could only leave the cave when the country had need of their help. Now was the time.

More cheers as people jumped onto the tables. John Kett wondered if all this fuss was necessary. It might be simple enough to find Granny and make her give the Taoiseach back. He was sure that Garrett was going overboard, especially when he began to shout, "To arms! To arms!"

Suddenly the cave was a frenzy of excitement. People were pulling out swords and spears and taking down old bits of armour.

"This crowd is getting very excited," John Kett said to James. They looked at Garrett, who had suddenly gone quiet.

A moment ago, he had been the chief rabble-rouser but now he looked thoughtful.

"There's only one problem," he said.

"What's that?" asked James.

"Horses!" said Garrett.

"Horses?" asked James.

"We need more horses!" said Garrett. "We only have three."

"If you could call them horses," thought Joan, looking towards the nags in the corner.

"We have only three horses," repeated Garrett. He paused for a moment and then said, "Only three of us can go."

"What are we going to do with this lot?" asked John Kett, watching the mayhem in the cave. Some had knives clenched in their teeth. Others were banging swords on the table and strapping on armour. Things were really getting out of hand.

Garrett didn't answer.

"Do you think the horses are a good idea?" John Kett asked. "I mean, it's a long way to Dublin. Couldn't we go by bus?"

"Distance means nothing to these noble animals," Garrett said. "You, me and Ruairí the Gallowglass will travel."

Ruairí looked very pleased to have been chosen. John Kett wasn't so pleased. Ruairí wore a coat of mail and carried a huge sword over one shoulder. A long bow and arrows were tucked under his arm. Altogether, he looked very fierce.

"What about us?" asked James. The children stood around looking defiant.

"Oh, you can come too," Garrett said. "These fine horses will also carry a child."

"Yipee-aye-ae," Frank shouted at the thought of a horse ride. John Kett wasn't at all sure.

It's madness, he thought, setting out on horses at this time of night. How could they see the road?

He tried again, "We could fit most of these people aboard the bus." Then he had second thoughts when he thought of driving such an armed and dangerous mob through the countryside in the dark.

Luckily, Garrett hadn't heard him and was now pulling the horses to the entrance of the cave. The "noble animals" looked spiritless and hungry.

"Now, my beauties, are we ready to take flight?" Garrett asked.

It took some time to saddle up. It had been years since Garrett and Ruairí had mounted a horse. Old bones creaked loudly. John Kett and the children hadn't ridden before and finally managed to sit the right way round. Frank was so excited he couldn't speak.

They looked out into the starry spring night. The lights of the market town twinkled in the distance. The air was still and the moon had risen over the brow of the hill. Garrett pointed to the moon. "Look – a light to guide us," he said

We'll need it, thought John Kett.

The grassy bank below fell away steeply from the entrance

to the cave. John Kett dreaded the thought of the downhill ride. Garrett was in marvellous form. His hour had come at last.

"It is time," he yelled and suddenly they were off into the night. As they lurched forward John Kett shut his eyes and held on tightly. Frank sat behind him, his arms clasped firmly around his dad's waist.

John Kett thought it strange that the horses were finding the path so easy. It was amazing that they were so sure-footed. He hadn't felt a jolt or a bump since they left the cave. It was almost as if they were flying through the air. He opened his eyes and quickly shut them again.

"Oh no!" he yelled. "We ARE!!" His stomach sank and he gripped even tighter. The horses were flying through the night sky.

The moonlight shone on the fields below them. They flew over hedges, meadows, farmhouses and hay-sheds.

"Don't look down!" he shouted to the children. "It's too frightening. You might fall off."

"Keep your hair on, Dad. This is great fun!" James roared back at him.

"This is better than the rollercoaster last summer,"

whooped Joan. By now she had changed her mind about the horses, and even about Garrett. Perhaps he was right when he called them "noble animals". Frank said nothing but gripped his dad tighter. His dad tightened his grasp on the horse's neck.

On they flew, over houses and church spires.

"There's the Boyne river," James yelled. The river was a silver ribbon in the moonlight.

"Follow it to the sea and then along the coast until we come to the city," James shouted.

John Kett began to relax. He could now open his eyes and wasn't afraid of falling off any more.

They dipped lower and followed the path of the river. They passed over weirs and bridges and flew between wooded banks. Nesting swans looked up and wild ducks quacked as they passed over.

Passing over the large town near the coast they sighted a large metal railway bridge on huge stone pillars that spanned the river. They waved at the train passing overhead as they swooped under the bridge. The passengers in the carriages changed sides to see their flight. The train rocked with the sudden movement and then continued on its way.

"Turn right at the sea," James directed. They travelled over the sand dunes at the mouth of the river and then followed the sandy beaches along the coast. The waves gently lapped the sands below and the moon carved a path across the sea. A yellow glow in the southern sky told them that they were approaching the city and their journey's end.

"How will we find the place?" Garrett shouted.

"It has a large dome roof with a clock," John Kett replied, "and it's always lit up like a Christmas tree." Garrett had never seen a Christmas tree before.

Now, as well as rescuing the Taoiseach, he could look forward to seeing, for the first time, a building that looked like a tree.

CHAPTER THIRTEEN
Lights, Cameras, Action!

The Taoiseach found it difficult to get out of the lift. He could either stay there all night or climb through the trapdoor in the ceiling. He could hear people scurrying around on top and he decided that The Nod had thrown a party as soon as he got him out of the room.

"The villain," he swore. "I bet he switched off the lift to keep me away from the hooley." He could hear activity in the street outside.

"I'll teach him to throw a party," he muttered to himself as he struggled to climb up to the trapdoor. He managed to step onto a rail mid-way on the wall and hoisted himself with great difficulty through the ceiling. He was in foul humour when he finally squeezed through the service hatch that opened into the kitchen.

"Nod, where are you, you party-pooper?" he roared.

There was no reply.

"When the cat's away, I suppose?" he called again.

He peeped into his office and to his surprise it was empty.

He scowled and looked around. He noticed a smoking cigar in the ashtray on his desk.

"The thievin' prat," he swore.

He spied the empty space on the coat-stand and his mouth dropped open.

"My... my coat is gone," he stuttered.

He stamped his foot.

"I might have guessed! The Nod always wanted that coat. I bet he's out swanning around the town pretending he's me. I'll fix him," he said.

As soon as he could find his glasses, he would go

downstairs immediately and report the theft of his coat to the security guard.

His glasses had disappeared too.

"I bet The Nod took them as well," he swore under his breath.

He looked again at the empty space on the coat-stand.

"Drat," he said. "It's chilly out there. I can't go out again without a coat."

He spied The Nod's old anorak. It was a sad-looking garment. It had been bought in a sale fifteen years ago, and looked it.

"I've told him to get rid of this rag a hundred times," he said to himself. He had refused to be seen in public with The Nod, who was almost as famous for wearing the anorak as the Taoiseach was for his coat with the velvet collar.

"Beggars can't be choosers," he said slipping on the anorak. He headed down the corridor. Rounding the top of the stairs he caught a glimpse of movement at the bottom. He leaned across the handrail. Without his glasses, it was difficult to see properly.

It appeared that three figures were crawling out from under the stairs. Two of them were dressed in some sort of uniform and the other had a bag over his head. Horror of horrors, but the one with the bag must be The Nod and he was wearing his lovely coat. He was dumbfounded. He must have that coat back. It was obviously some criminal group that The Nod had joined.

"The bag over his head is a poor disguise. I'd recognise the paunch anywhere," he scoffed. He decided to tail them, but he had to be careful as they might be armed.

The Nod shuffled along between the criminals as they made their way towards the courtyard. The Taoiseach slunk along behind them, tight to the wall.

The criminals burst through the doors and ran across the open space. The Taoiseach watched from behind a huge pillar under the porch.

Guards poured from the security hut and ran after the trio. There was no escape. They were surrounded. Moonlight glinted on the guards' gun barrels. A crackle was heard as a loudspeaker system was switched on.

"Stop or we fire!" it boomed.

The Taoiseach knew that the game was up. He hoped that The Nod would have the good sense to surrender before his coat was riddled with bullet holes.

He could see that they were desperate. It was only a matter of minutes before they surrendered. How could The Nod ever have thought he would get away with this daft exploit? Suddenly everybody was looking up and pointing towards the sky. The guards had jumped to their feet and looked uneasy. The criminals also stared upwards. The Taoiseach saw movement on the skyline above the buildings. He thought he saw a horse drop out of the sky.

He shut his eyes and moved back behind the column.

"I blame this on being stuck in the lift and losing my

glasses," he laughed, "and all this nonsense with The Nod and the coat. Horses from the sky indeed!" He chuckled loudly and looked out again. Another horse dropped from the sky. He closed his eyes tight and opened them again. Three horses and riders were standing in the courtyard facing The Nod and the two women criminals. The security guards stood behind them scratching their heads. The arrival of the horses had taken them by surprise and they didn't know what to do. Each of the riders had a child sitting behind them. Some wore old-fashioned clothes and looked very fierce indeed.

Then it came to him suddenly. He knew exactly what was happening.

"They're making a film!" he gasped.

The Nod had arranged to use the

courtyard as a location for a new film. It was something called *Up With the Wind*. Of course, this was it. Horses dropping out of the sky indeed. They were making a film and The Nod was starring in it. He was obviously playing the hero, dressed as him, the Taoiseach. That's why he had stolen his coat. He became angry. Why, he could have starred in the film himself, wearing his own coat. He had the talent, the looks, the charisma. The Nod didn't even look like him. He was short of height, looks and everything. He must put a stop to this at once. He ran into the courtyard, shouting, "Wait, it should have been me!"

The horsemen saw him running towards them. John Kett shouted, "Watch out, there's a thug in an old anorak running towards the Taoiseach. Save him, Ruairí."

"Save who?" asked Ruairí, not knowing who was who.

"The one in the coat with the bag on his head, he's the Taoiseach," John Kett shouted back. "I'd recognise the coat anywhere."

"He is not," replied the "thug" in the old anorak running towards them. "I'm the real Taoiseach, and I want my coat back!" He streaked across the courtyard towards Nod and the ladies.

James was unsure but didn't like the look of this would-be assassin. He could have a knife concealed under that old coat. Trust Granny to get them into this spot of danger.

"Hy..app!" he shouted as he the belted the nag on the flank. The horse shot forward and as it passed the real Taoiseach, James dived.

It was a perfect tackle. The Taoiseach was instantly winded and sank to the ground.

James jumped up.

"Quick, rescue the Taoiseach," he shouted to Ruairí, "before another thug tries to maim him. There'll be more of them hiding somewhere." The real Taoiseach lay moaning on the ground.

Quick as a flash, Ruairí galloped towards The Nod and reaching down grabbed him around his plump waist. Lifting him, he threw him, bottom up, across the horse's neck. The guards, recovering from the shock of the dropping horses, began to move in around them.

"We must be off," roared Garrett, seeing that they were in danger.

"James, get back up on your horse," John Kett shouted.

"There's no room," James yelled. "Save the Taoiseach. I'll try and help Granny."

The real Taoiseach, now recovered, was furious and struggled to his feet.

"Arrest everybody," he roared. "This is treason!"

To think that this was all happening in his own government buildings! One by one, he saw the horses leap upwards into the sky.

"Amazing," he thought, "what they can do with wires! These special effects are marvellous," he mused. Then he spied the brat who had tackled him. A sly-looking ruffian if ever he saw one. He was shaking the two old criminals. They seemed to be in a state of shock as if they hadn't expected the horses to leap into the sky. "That's real acting," he thought admiringly. Then he checked and asked himself, "Are they actors or criminals?"

It was all very confusing. He decided to give chase in case they were either or both, and besides, they would know where The Nod and his own lovely coat had gone.

James looked around and saw the security guards running towards them. There was no escape, except back through the building.

"Quick, Granny, Mrs Strong, back inside at once. We're all in trouble," he yelled. He pushed the stunned ladies ahead through the doors. They were in a daze. The Taoiseach was close behind followed by the guards. They ran up the stairs. In spite of their state of shock, James was surprised as to how fast the ladies could run, but then of course this was a matter of life and death. At the top of the stairs, he glanced back to see the Taoiseach gasping for breath halfway up the steps.

"Good," he thought, "that'll give us a few minutes."

They made it to the top floor ahead of the posse and charged down the corridor. The ladies were magnificent. They streaked ahead and James was hard put to keep up with them. To their dismay, they found that the door was locked at the end of the corridor. When it wouldn't budge with a strong rattle, panic almost set in. Then Mrs Strong spied an open window. She stuck her head through to investigate. It opened onto a wide ledge that overlooked the courtyard. The Taoiseach turned the corner and they knew the security guards were right behind. There was nothing for it but to climb out onto the ledge. Mrs Strong went first, followed by Granny and then James. They edged their way along, not daring to look down.

Refreshed by the chase the ladies were in excellent form.

"Move over, pigeons," Mrs Strong quipped as they sidled along. They hopped lightly over roosting pigeons as if they were stepping over puddles. Only James was struggling.

A head appeared at a window further back. It was the Taoiseach.

"Are they actors or criminals?" he asked himself again. "Either way, they probably know where my coat has gone... Onward!" Suddenly he realised that by following these actor criminals he might be caught on film at any moment. Perhaps this might even be his chance to show The Nod how he could play the leading man and run along a dangerous ledge?

He smiled into the night, and perhaps at the cameras, as he stepped onto the ledge. He took two steps, looked down and froze. The courtyard looked a long way below.

"Help," he chirped.

James looked back. The assassin in the old anorak had followed them out onto the ledge. He could see that he was in trouble. He was about to go back when the thought struck him that it might be a trick.

"Can't take the chance. He'd probably stick a knife in my ribs."

Granny and Mrs Strong had moved ahead to where the ledge widened and curved upwards. Mrs Strong called back, "We can't go any further. There's a big gap here. The only way from here is down."

"Can we climb down?" asked Granny, already tucking the end of her skirt into her knickers.

"I think so, if we're careful," answered Mrs Strong.

The exploit that followed should rank alongside the descent of Mount Everest. Using the crooks of their umbrellas and pure determination, the ladies, followed by James, made their way down the face of the building. They swung from the umbrellas, wedged themselves between walls and toe-gripped recesses. Mrs Strong was the first to land. A short time later, all three stood under an archway leading to a side street. This was the only way out. They were about to bolt when they heard a pitiful cry, "Help, get me down."

"What's that?" asked Granny.

"It's that thug who tried to attack us in the courtyard," answered James.

"The old fogey, I don't know what makes people climb out on dangerous ledges. He should have more sense at his age," said Granny.

"Serves him right. Best to leave him there," said Mrs Strong.

Suddenly security guards streamed out of the building and gathered under the ledge where the "thug" was stranded. The trio stepped back into the shadows and watched. With sirens blazing, a fire brigade turned into the courtyard. Firemen tumbled out and pulled a large rescue net which looked like a big trampoline.

A strong spotlight was trained on the Taoiseach.

Blinded for a moment, he backed tightly against the wall.

"I'm being filmed," he gasped. Any second now he would hear, "Lights, camera, action!" This was his big chance. He looked down at the trampoline. They expected him to jump. He only hesitated for a moment. Of course, lesser film-stars would need a stand-in, but not him.

He smiled into the glare of the lights and waited. The director would shout instructions at any moment.

A security guard appeared at the window behind him and asked, "Can you make your way back, Taoiseach?"

"Make my way back?" he hissed. "If The Nod can disappear into the sky on the back of a horse, I can jump into a sheet. My public expect it of me."

He could see the large red dot on the trampoline below. He waited. The director would be sitting somewhere out of sight, in the dark.

"What's keeping him?" asked Mrs Strong. "We'll be here all night."

Granny smirked and cupped her hands to her mouth.

"Jump, ya big galoot!" she yelled.

"The instruction, at last," sighed the Taoiseach, who had only heard the "jump" call.

He straightened up and stepped forward to the edge.

"Lesser mortals jump," he said, "but I'll show them."

He braced himself and launched into the most graceful and surprising swallow dive that the firemen had ever seen a Taoiseach perform. He glided through the air and landed safely. He bounced to his feet at once. Surprisingly, there was no applause, only silence broken by the odd giggle.

The security guards had heard Granny's "jump" call and ran to investigate.

The trio took to their heels and bolted through the gateway which, fortunately for them, had been left open.

CHAPTER FOURTEEN
A Terrible Time

When The Nod was hoisted across Ruairí's horse he thought that his end had finally come. He had never had such a terrible time in all his life. It was bad enough to be kidnapped by ruthless terrorists, but to be thrown across a horse and galloped off into the night was even worse. Besides, he hated horses since he was a child, when one had thought that his fingers were part of a sugar lump.

He was relieved for a moment when the bag slipped off his

head. He blinked a few times to try and focus as the sight of street lights and traffic below made him imagine that he must be airborne. The fright of his capture must have unhinged him.

"This is a horse, and horses don't fly," he said as he opened and shut his eyes. Perhaps it was all a nightmare and he would wake up slumped in the Taoiseach's chair at any moment. The traffic looked like small bright dots moving along the roads. He winced. He was having the most terrible time he could ever remember. He looked up at his captor and gulped. Ruairí looked fierce, his teeth clenched, his chain-mail rattling in the wind, and hung about with frightful looking weapons. The Nod was certain that he was being carted off to some grim place where he would be ritually butchered. His other captors and their children pillion-riders waved at him. A thin, damp-looking man with a small girl behind, edged his horse alongside and said, "Welcome aboard, Taoiseach. You are safe with us."

"Hah," The Nod thought to himself. "Safe, am I?"

How could he be safe a thousand feet up in the air, suspended across the neck of a bony nag? Safe was having two feet on the ground or sitting on his chair in the office. He felt ill and clamped his hand over his mouth.

Ruairí patted his back.

"It's called being air sick," he said with understanding. "You'll get used to flying. There's normally a bag under the saddle, but as we're over the sea you won't need it."

The beauty of the night flight was lost on The Nod who saw nothing of the moonlight shining on the sea. He also missed the view over the river as they travelled back to Hacklim. He got sick over the estuary as they turned inland and he remembered nothing more of the journey until they landed on a hillside outside a brightly-lit cave. He knew by the boisterous sounds coming from within that he had reached the place of his execution. The pagan celebration was being prepared and he guessed he was to be their sacrifice. He had read how victims were dragged through the crowd and slaughtered to wild cheers.

A delicious smell of roasting beef wafted through the air.

"Their last victim," The Nod thought and sweat formed on his brow.

"Well, that was great," said Frank. "I thought that we'd never escape from all those guards. That bit was real scary."

"Oh, I bet the guards were just as scared. Especially when they saw your face," teased Joan

"Cop on," said Frank. John Kett, sensing that a row was brewing, said, "Not in front of the Taoiseach, children." He smiled towards The Nod, and noticed the beads of perspiration on his forehead.

"What's that smell?" said Joan sniffing the air.

The others dismounted, and eyed each other.

Garrett was annoyed. "That's a roasting cow," he scowled. "The divil take the gallowglasses, but there's been a cattle raid." He was right. As they entered the cave to riotous sounds they could see a whole cow being cooked on a spit over the fire. The cook was busy hacking off lumps of meat and sending steaming platters to the tables. The gallowglasses grabbed handfuls of meat and crammed them into their mouths. It was then washed down with plentiful cups of a red drink. The noisy gathering looked very happy indeed.

Two more cows were tied in the corner and John Kett supposed that they were tomorrow's meals.

He knew there would be trouble when the missing cattle were discovered.

Garrett felt it was time to welcome the Taoiseach. He was sure that the meat would provide an excellent meal for his guest.

He took the nervous-looking Nod by the arm and led him through the crowd towards the chair. Never having seen such a beautiful coat, curious greasy fingers reached out to touch him. The Nod hopped and swerved to avoid the fingers of the murderous rabble. He prayed that he would soon wake up from this terrible nightmare. Garrett sat The Nod in the big chair and stood beside him. The Ketts and Fingers watched.

"He doesn't look right to me," said Fingers, staring at The Nod.

"What do you mean?" asked Joan.

"There's something wrong with him. I've seen the Taoiseach on TV... The coat is right, but..."

"Maybe he got his hair cut," said John Kett. "It can make you look quite different. Why, I remember one time when I came back from the barbers..."

"A thousand years ago," said Joan, looking at his bald head. Garrett rose to speak.

"Silence, my people," he demanded from the platform.

The crowd hushed. The Nod chewed his nails.

"This is the Taoiseach. The esteemed and great leader of our country." The Nod looked uncomfortable. He glanced up, twitched his face and stared straight ahead. The crowd looked uneasy. The gallowglasses wondered if "great and esteemed" was a fitting description for somebody who sat hunched in the chair, staring into space.

"We have rescued him from scheming kidnappers and assassins, in the courtyard of his very own palace."

The crowd cheered as Garrett continued, "He will remain here until it is safe to return."

The Nod listened carefully. He liked the bit about the palace. Very fitting, he thought. It crossed his mind that as long as they thought he was the Taoiseach it was unlikely that the murderous rabble would rise up and cut his throat.

Already he could feel the coat giving him confidence. He straightened up and stuck out his chin.

"Something to drink for our honoured guest," ordered Garrett, clapping his hands. A smiling serving maid sauntered over carrying a big jug. She poured him a large glass of the red drink which he gulped back quickly. He blinked and thrust his glass forward again.

"I'll have some of that," said Frank, seeing that The Nod had enjoyed his drink so much.

"Children don't drink mead!" Garrett said. "You'll

enjoy some nice warm milk from one of the captured cows."

Frank wasn't so sure when he saw the same serving maid roll up her sleeves, sit under the cow and squirt steaming, hissing milk into a bowl.

"Jumpin' giblets," said Joan under her breath. "I hope they're not going to make me drink that."

"I only drink milk from a bottle or a carton," she announced, deciding she would have nothing to do with anything that came directly from a live animal. The girl set the bowl of milk in front of Frank. Joan smirked as Frank stared at the warm milk.

Meanwhile, The Nod had swilled back his third cup of mead. He was feeling warm inside. He was beginning to enjoy being Taoiseach. His cheeks glowed.

Chapter Fifteen

Night Frights

Granny, James and Mrs Strong ran through the archway and out on to a narrow street. Both ends of the street were blocked and for a moment it seemed that there was no way out.

"Let's stay calm," Granny ordered as she looked around.

Mrs Strong glanced anxiously through the archway. She could see the crowd milling around the Taoiseach. To her surprise he was still jumping up and down on the trampoline. The firemen were finding it difficult to get him to step off. He could be there for some time. As she watched, two security guards detached themselves from the crowd and ran towards them.

"They're coming for us. We've got to get out of here quick," she urged.

"Don't lose your cool, Strong," Granny advised.

"Right on, Granny," James smiled. He spotted an open window in the building on the opposite side of the street.

"This way," he whispered. He tugged at them and ran across the street.

Earlier that day a grille with iron bars had been removed to allow workmen to remove rubbish through a window. It had been left unlocked and James pushed up the sash without any trouble.

"Quick, climb in, ladies," he ordered.

"Do you think we should?" Granny asked, peering into the dark inside. "Won't somebody mind?"

"This coming from the woman who has just tried to kidnap the Taoiseach," he thought.

"We'll all mind if they arrest us for kidnapping," he said

angrily. "Get in quick."

The sound of running feet came from the courtyard as the ladies struggled through the window. Grunting like small pigs they fell on top of each other inside.

"Careful, Strong," Granny threatened and pinched sharply. Mrs Strong squealed. James slipped though – only a moment before the security guards arrived on the street outside.

"Have you ever broken into a building before, Strong?" asked Granny, brushing herself down. Mrs Strong thought for a moment and then answered, "Well, one time my cat got locked in a telephone kiosk..."

"Shsssh," James said. "Stop gabbling." He thought that their chattering would attract the guards at any moment.

To his relief they stopped, obviously resigned to suffer in silence.

From the side of the window he watched the guards who looked around and then scratched their heads. Puzzled at the sudden disappearance of their quarry, they hung around for a few minutes and wandered back through the arch.

"Phew," said James. "Safe for the moment."

"It's very dusty in here," said Granny, sneezing.

"And dark," said Mrs Strong.

"Get your torch out then," said Granny.

"I almost forgot," tittered Mrs Strong as she searched for her carrier bag in the dark. She located it and began to rummage for the flashlight.

"Mobile telephone, sandwiches, flask..." she said as if she had discovered the contents of her bag for the first time.

"Flask!" said Granny. "Marvellous, I could do with a cup of tea."

"Tea – at a time like this!" thought James, glancing nervously towards the street.

"Careful with the torch," he warned. "Someone might see the light."

The ladies managed to drink their tea in the darkness.

They stiffened from time to time when they heard a noise outside. It was as if someone was searching up and down.

"Probably a tramp looking for a place to sleep," Granny whispered.

The tea was luke warm but nevertheless, after the exhausting chase, it was welcome. Sucking her teeth, Granny said, "Well, we can't stay here all night. Where are we anyhow?"

Mrs Strong fumbled for the torch and switched it on. A beam of yellow light cut through the darkness.

"Merciful grief!" shrieked Granny

"Agggh!" screamed Mrs Strong and dropped the torch at once. The light went out.

"Did you see it?" blubbered Granny

"It was horrible," wailed Mrs Strong.

"The devil himself."

"A huge skull with wings."

"Let's get out of here."

"But it's out there... waiting for us."

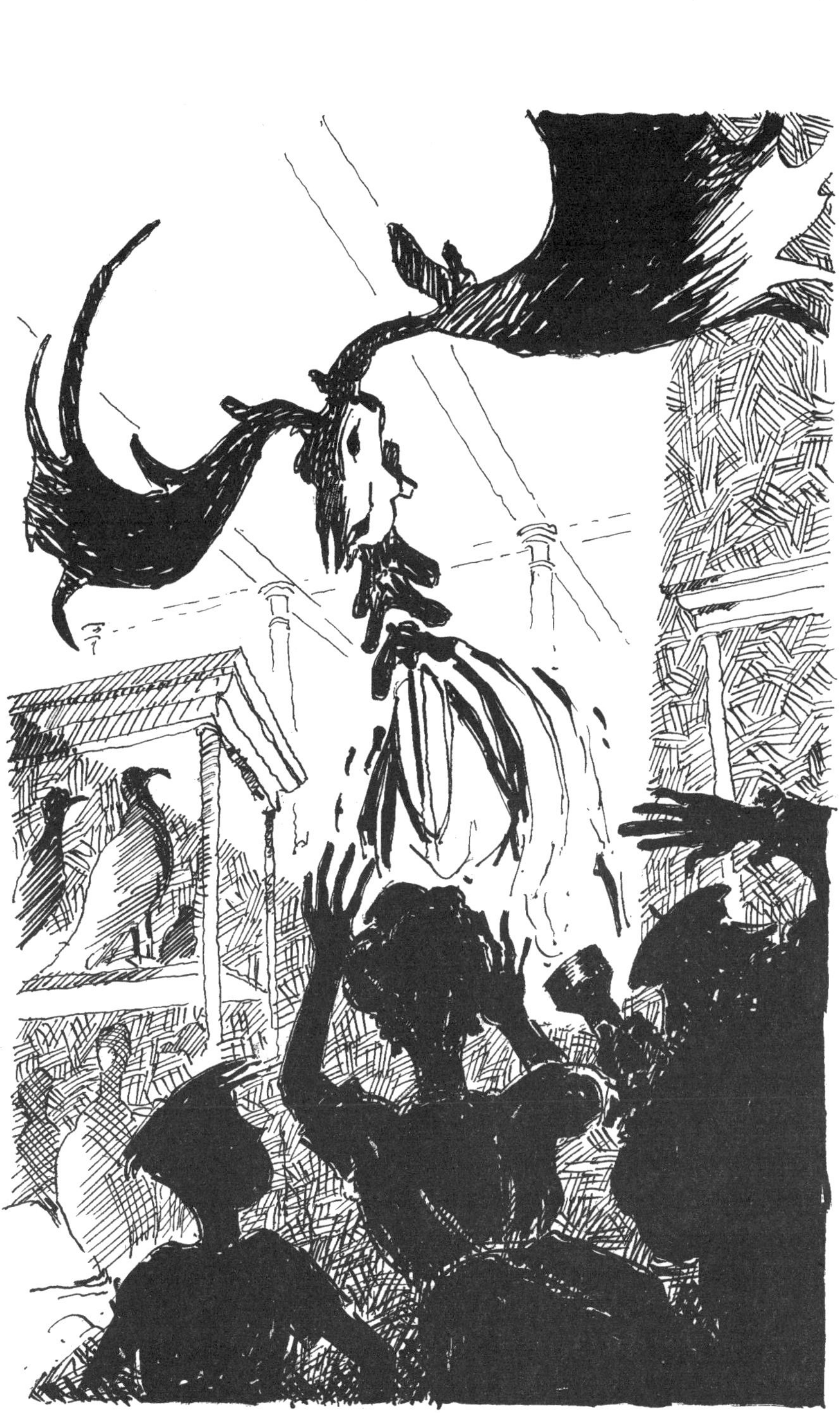

The ladies hugged each other and as much as he tried James couldn't get a word in edgeways.

"We're finished, Strong."

"Never believed in this sort of thing, until now."

"Oh, help!"

"Oh, mercy!"

"STOP, LADIES, STOP!" James raised his voice. There were lights and noises outside the window now. The torch light had attracted attention. The ladies whimpered quietly.

"There's nothing to be afraid of," he said. "We're in the Natural History Museum. It's a place where they exhibit skeletons of animals... and rocks and things. Dad has brought us here before."

"Well, just like that man to bring children to a weird place like this. It's unhealthy if you ask me!" said Mrs Strong

"Nobody's asking you," said Granny, beginning to pull herself together. Mrs Strong felt like sulking.

"What did we see out there?" Granny asked James.

"It was the skeleton of the Giant Irish Deer. It's called 'Megaceros'. They died out a long time ago."

"I'm not surprised," said Granny, "probably frightened themselves to death."

Lights were now shining through the windows. The torch light had attracted attention.

"We've got to move," said James. "We'll try and find somewhere to hide until they go away."

"Hide in here?" protested Granny, "with all these skeletons. Why, it's like an animals' graveyard."

"I suppose it is a sort of animals' graveyard," said James

"Weird, if you ask me," said Mrs Strong, sounding very huffy. "They'll find us, lifeless, huddled in some corner, with wide staring eyes."

"Make tracks," said Granny in a no-nonsense voice.

They moved off and picked their way through endless display cases containing stuffed animals and birds of every description. The light from the windows occasionally glinted on the glass eye of a stuffed fox or wolf and made them look ghastly and frightening.

At every corner Mrs Strong felt her heart flutter as yet another stuffed exhibit gazed out from their glass case. The great crested grebe with its little stuffed chicks almost made her cry.

She felt the otter stared accusingly as if she had trapped him in his timeless glass box.

"They're very dead, Strong," Granny would say on hearing her gasp.

They bumped their way around in the half darkness. James gave up using the torch. Apart from attracting attention it lit up exhibits that frightened the ladies.

There were screams when the light caught the skeleton of the giant ground sloth.

"It's only the megatherium," he said reassuringly.

The stuffed rhinoceros produced a squeal and the hippopotamus a muffled shriek.

Finally he put the torch away when the suspended skeleton of the common rorqual whale was caught by its beam. Mrs Strong screeched and clasped her hands over her head.

"It moved," she yelled, "I swear it did."

"It's either the draught or your imagination," said Granny, a little unsure herself.

The massive bony skeleton of the whale hanging from the roof glared threateningly at them.

"This is a terrible place," whimpered Mrs Strong. "Can't we get out of it?" But it was too late. Even as she spoke they heard the sound of the door opening and footsteps running through the ground floor of the building. They were on the top floor and were staring eye to eye socket with the skull of the whale.

James knew they were trapped and that they would soon be discovered. They were on a high balcony overlooking the exhibits on the upstairs floor. Large stuffed animals peered above the top of the cases. The stuffed elephant and giraffe stood strangely silent. The search party hadn't got this far yet.

Granny spied an almost empty display case at the end of the balcony. "We could hide in there," she said.

"Hide in a glass case?" gasped Mrs Strong.

"We'll look like another exhibit."

Granny saw the look of disbelief on James' face.

"There's plenty of old animal skins hanging about. We'll wrap them around us, place a few stuffed monkeys at the front and Bob's your uncle."

The animal skins were indeed old and smelled dreadful. The stuffed monkeys smelled just as bad. They wrapped the skins around them, positioned the monkeys with a few withered plants in between. Although the smell was terrible, Granny was pleased with the arrangement. Sitting on stools, they peered through the decaying shrubs.

Suddenly lights were switched on and the building was fully lit. Guards checked every nook and cranny. Fortunately for Granny and her friends their display case was in part shadow.

James saw Granny stiffen. She was watching something on the floor below.

"That thug is here," she hissed out of the side of her mouth.

"What thug? Where?" asked Mrs Strong.

"The one who chased us and then jumped off the ledge," answered Granny.

"Oh, the madman who tried to murder the Taoiseach before he was mercifully whisked off," nodded Mrs Strong.

To their amazement the thug was giving orders and the guards scurried everywhere as if he was someone of importance. Two guards were dispatched to their balcony. The trio froze when they stopped outside their case.

"I think this one's new, Fred," one said peering through the glass.

"Amazing, the things they find out there," Fred answered, shaking his head.

"The one in the middle looks quite vicious," the first one said, looking straight at Granny.

"It looks really angry."

"I wouldn't like to meet it in real life."

"Best left out in the jungle."

They moved on. Granny felt her nose begin to twitch. The awful-smelling fur was tickling it. She couldn't stop herself.

"Atishoo!" she sneezed.

The guards spun around. "What was that, Fred?" one asked. They glanced around suspiciously.

"Probably nothing. These stuffed exhibits build up gases and blow from time to time. Like a puncture."

The other nodded and they moved on.

"Like a puncture," sniggered Mrs Strong.

Granny glared. "Build up gases indeed!"

"The mobile phone," said James.

"No, I sneezed, " said Granny

"Why didn't I think of it before?" James said "The mobile phone. We'll try and contact Dad. He'll get us out of here, somehow."

Mrs Strong rummaged and found the tea flask as well as the phone. While James attempted to contact his dad the ladies had another cup of tea.

He couldn't get a reply on their home phone and guessed that his dad was back in Hacklim with his mum. He telephoned the cottage and to his delight his mother answered.

"Hi Mum," he said. "Can you get a message to Dad at the cave?"

He had a lot of explaining to do. His mother had hardly heard of the cave and he had to start from scratch.

"Where are you now?" she asked.

"I'm in the Museum of Natural History with Granny and Mrs Strong."

"The what?" asked his mother.

"It's the place where they keep old bones and stuffed animals." he answered.

"Speaking of old bones, did you say Granny's there?" she asked.

"Yes," he said, reluctantly.

"Can I talk to her?" she asked. "I can't find her brown bread recipe. I want to ask her if it's milk or buttermilk?"

"Look Mum, we're under pressure. Make it short."

"*You're* under pressure?" his mother replied. "I have to bake six loaves of brown bread for the school cake stall."

An extraordinary phone call followed. Oven temperatures were discussed and whether it was best to use wheat or bran. When the conversation moved on to tips on playing bridge, James grabbed the phone. Granny, enjoying the chat, looked peeved. "Look Mum, we're in trouble," said James. "Dad and his friends will have to rescue us. Tell them to meet us on the roof. It's the only way out – and hurry."

He had just finished his call when he detected a movement from the side of his eye. Phone in hand, he froze. Granny and Mrs Strong also became motionless. Granny had been sipping from a cup of tea which remained fixed in front of her face. James sat rigid, the mobile phone in his fist. Mrs Strong was bent over her hand trapped in her plastic carrier bag.

The Taoiseach stood in front of the display case staring at the exhibit. He had taken full charge and was intent on flushing out the criminals, or actors or whatever they might be. Granny wondered what this thug was doing in the building. Whoever he was, he could give the game away if they as much as moved a finger. The Taoiseach slowly circled the case.

Puzzled, he stared at the collection of exhibits. The monkeys looked real enough and the big creature on the outside looked quite fierce. Why was it wearing spectacles, he wondered, and delving into what looked like a modern carrier bag? Strange how modern merchandise had invaded the far flung lairs of even these creatures. The big hairy one in the middle had been made to appear to drink from a modern-looking cup. Strangest of all, the smallest one was holding a mobile phone. Was nothing sacred? he thought. Must these unfortunates adopt the worst gadgets of our modern society? He probably traded it in for a priceless piece of hand-worked jewellery, handed down from father to son for generations.

How thought-provoking these exhibits were. He must make a note to congratulate whoever had put the display together.

"Marvellous," he said and turned to go. Trying to hold her breath, Granny was turning blue., They all drew a deep breath as the Taoiseach moved away.

"Bleep, Bleep," the mobile phone rang.

No one moved. Amazed, the Taoiseach turned around.

"Bleep, Bleep," the phone continued and a little red light flashed.

Keeping his eye on the dumbstruck Taoiseach, James lifted the phone and slowly said, "Hello."

"Oh James, this is your mother," the voice replied. "I'm off now to the cave and tell Granny I found the brown bread recipe. Byeee." The line went dead.

Without moving his lips, James said. "Gather up your belongings, smile at the man, and when I say 'Go', bolt for the door!"

Granny, James and Mrs Strong rose to their feet, removed the smelly pelts while smiling and nodding at the speechless Taoiseach.

"Go," shouted James, and they were off like bats out of hell. The had disappeared through the door and were halfway up the stairs leading to the roof when the Taoiseach came to. It was the first time in his life that he had been talked to by stuffed exhibits, actors and criminals all at once.

"What next?" he asked himself as he took to his heels and gave chase.

Chapter Sixteen

Meanwhile, Back at the Cave...

Meanwhile, back in the cave in Hacklim, The Nod was having the time of his life. His fortunes had completely changed. Instead of the worst, he was now having the best time he could ever remember. The more mead he drank the more he relaxed. Keenan the bard stuck up a praise song, composed on the spot. It told of The Nod's heroic deeds in avoiding the assassin in the courtyard and how he had jumped ten metres into the air onto the back of a flying horse. As the night wore on the height of the jump increased to fifty metres and the song also told of how he had wiped out twenty assassins at a single sword stroke. The song was boring to everybody except The Nod. Soon he believed the exploits himself. He laughed when the gallowglasses threw things at Keenan. Enjoying the fun, he joined in the game, throwing plates and cups across the room. The place was in an uproar.

"Time to go home," said John Kett as he ducked to avoid another plate.

"Ah, not yet, Dad, this man is terribly funny," said Frank.

The Nod was now standing on the table in the centre of the room.

"Shhh," he said, waving his hands about. "Quiet, I want to tell a joke." A milk jug whizzed past his ear. He reached down and pulled the serving maid up beside him.

"You've just milked a cow," he said, "but tell me, how do you get milk from a cat?" The serving maid looked puzzled.

"It's easy," he roared, "you steal its saucer!"

He slapped his hands on his knees and roared laughing at his own joke. Some of the gallowglasses laughed along with him but most of the crowd, except for Frank, couldn't see the joke. That didn't bother The Nod who was now in full flight.

"A man went to the doctor and said, 'I want something for wind,'" he roared, bending over and pointing at the crowd. 'Here's a kite,' the doctor said!" he roared. Frank laughed so much he thought his sides would split.

The Nod was unstoppable and didn't care whether anybody listened or laughed. He was clearly enjoying himself. He managed to avoid a flying table leg and continued with the next joke.

Garrett turned to John Kett. "A surprising way for the esteemed and great leader of the country to act."

John Kett nodded, uneasy himself at The Nod's behaviour.

"Are you sure he is the real leader?" Garrett asked.

"Well he's wearing the right coat," John Kett replied.

The Nod was now walking on his hands, upside-down, along the table. He swerved over and back and even in this position, showed great skill at avoiding missiles. The crowd loved this and shouted their encouragement.

"Thank goodness, I've found you," a voice behind them said. "Is this a circus?"

It was Mary Kett, who had finally found the cave.

John Kett smiled and Joan and Frank ran towards her.

They explained, as best they could, what was going on. She barely heard. She was fascinated by the cave and strolled about looking at this and that. Garrett was delighted to meet her again and show her around.

"Garrett," she said. "This place looks as if it hasn't been touched for centuries. You could do wonders in here with wallpaper!"

Garrett nodded thoughtfully.

"Put stripes on the bottom here and a nice flowery pattern on the top," she said.

In a short time they had decided on a complete colour scheme for the whole cave. Garrett looked pleased.

A jug splintered on the wall beside them.

"Shame about the crockery," she said and then remembered why she had come. She ran over to her husband John.

"With all this going on, I almost forgot. James telephoned. Granny, Mrs Strong and himself are in some sort of trouble."

"Where are they?" John Kett asked, wondering if he could manage the bail money.

"Let me think," she said. "On the roof of some place, with stuffed animals."

"What are they doing on a roof with stuffed animals?" asked Garrett.

"Are there stuffed animals on the roof?" she asked, "I thought they said they were inside along with a lot of old bones."

"It's the Museum of Natural History," said John Kett. "They must be trapped on the roof. We've got to get them down."

"Another rescue!" shouted Garrett with excitement. "Get the horses again."

The nags looked even sadder than before. The last flight had left them exhausted. They were finding it hard to sleep with the racket in the cave. The Nod had now taken to juggling plates for the entertainment of the crowd. Most of them landed on the floor.

"More like smashing than juggling," Joan said to Frank as the crockery fragmented on the floor. But The Nod was Frank's hero, and he laughed heartily at his antics.

"Hup-ho, my beauties," yelled Garrett at the unwilling nags. He pulled them to the door of the cave.

Much to Joan's disappointment, they decided to leave the children behind. Only John Kett, Garrett and one horse would travel. Frank didn't mind at all as he was enjoying The Nod's act.

John Kett turned to Mary, "If we're not back by first light you must drive the bus to the parade. Collect the Ancient Monuments Society on the way."

"Yes, dear," she nodded and he wondered if she had really heard. She too was watching The Nod who had grabbed Keenan's harp and was pretending to play it like a guitar. He was doing a bad Elvis imitation.

They took off into the night sky to the strains of "I went to a party in the county jail". The riotous sounds followed for a while. The Nod switched back to telling jokes and the crowd were as wild as ever. Frank laughed so much he fell off his chair.

"You're such a sad person," said Joan, but Frank didn't care.

CHAPTER SEVENTEEN

Waterworks

Granny, Mrs Strong and James knew the Taoiseach and the security guards weren't far behind as they chased up the narrow staircase leading to the roof. To their relief, they found a ladder against the wall, under a trapdoor on the top landing. "This must be the way up," James said. "It'll take a minute to get the ladder into position."

"They're right behind," said Granny, peering over the stairs. The thug from the courtyard appeared, closely followed by security guards.

"Hold them off until I get this ladder up," said James.

He pushed it under the roof light and climbed up.

Granny searched around for something to throw at their pursuers.

"Use this," yelled Mrs Strong pulling a hose-reel off the wall.

"Throw it at them?" shouted Granny. "We'll do more than that. Let's soak 'em." She pointed the nozzle down the stairs.

"Let it rip, Strong."

Midway in his flight up the stairs a gush of water hit the Taoiseach. He gasped, fell back and flattened the guards behind. Caught in the surge of water they tumbled down the stairs to land in a heap on the steps below.

"Quick, Granny," James shouted. "Up the ladder now."

"Must I?" she complained.

Granny was enjoying herself. She played the hose over the squirming Taoiseach and the squealing guards. Each time they stood up, the water jet knocked them down again.

"Treason, treason," the Taoiseach yelled.

Granny wondered why he was calling her Teresa. She hardly knew the man. You never knew with thugs these days.

"Not that we're on first name terms, but you can call me Gran!" shrieked Granny, letting go another blast.

"C'mon, Gran, you can't hold them off forever!" James yelled again.

"Wanna bet!" said Gran. "Shucks! Just as I was enjoying myself."

On the final burst the hose pulled away from the wall. Water spurted everywhere. Granny jumped onto the ladder to avoid the spray. She was about to throw the hose away until she thought.

"This might come in handy." She pulled it after her as she climbed through the trapdoor onto the roof.

"Hurry, Gran," James said as he helped her through. Mrs Strong was already sitting on the slates clutching her carrier bag. She looked very uncomfortable in the light from the street below.

James panted as he replaced the heavy cover over the trapdoor.

"Sit on this, will you, Mrs Strong? We need to stop them pushing it open again," he suggested with a smile.

Mrs Strong smiled back and carefully slid across the slates onto the cover.

"Thank you," James muttered, hoping that she didn't think he asked her to sit there because he thought she was heavy or anything like that.

Granny climbed further up the roof and peered through the glass roof over the exhibition hall below.

"They're scurrying around like rabbits down there," she said. The hall below was a hive of activity with more and more guards streaming up from the ground floor.

"Oh look," she said, "soldiers have arrived, with guns too. Imagine that." She chuckled, delighted with her bird's eye view.

James frowned. Things were getting worse. He hoped that their rescue wouldn't be long.

Mrs Strong was being bumped up and down. They were trying to push the roof-light cover from the underside. She held on tightly and smiled anxiously towards James.

"Hold out as long as you can, Mrs Strong," James urged.

"I'm afraid that if they rock me too much, I'll fall off the roof," she pleaded.

"Goodness, we can't allow that," he replied.

He looked around and spied the hose lying across the slates. He took one end and tied it around Mrs Strong's middle. The other end he lassoed around a pipe sticking through the roof.

"That should keep you safe," he said.

As Mrs Strong rocked to and fro on the roof-light a rosy glow appeared in the eastern sky. The dawn was breaking.

Chapter Eighteen
We'll All Go

Mary Kett was having problems getting them all on the bus. She certainly hadn't intended taking this wild lot with her. At the first light of dawn Joan had reminded her that it was time to leave for the National Parade. Frank was still enjoying The Nod and Joan thought that it was time she put a stop to that.

"Time to go, Mum," she said.

"Can we bring Garrett, please?" Frank asked.

"Well I'm sure Mr Fitzgerald has lots to do, tidying up this cave," she smiled. "And thinking about his wallpapering," she added, desperately.

"But you always say that tidying up can wait for another day," insisted Frank.

"But I'm sure Mr Fitzgerald and his friends want to pick up all the crockery and wash the pots before they go out," smiled Mary Kett walking away quickly.

"But I'd love to go," boomed Garrett.

"Me too," shouted Keenan the harpist.

"And me," roared Ruairí the gallowglass.

"Why don't we all go?" yelled a voice from the table. The Nod stood there, his arms spread wide to embrace the crowd.

He was midway through his tap dance. He had tied silver plates to the soles of his shoes and demonstrated a soft shoe shuffle on the table top. The gallowglasses were eating out of his hands and when he suggested that they all go on the bus there was a roar of approval from the floor. Although defeated, Mary Kett smiled through it all. Breeding always wins out.

She had little choice but to take all who chose to come. When she set off down the hill leading the jostling, singing crowd she felt like the Pied Piper. He probably felt much the same about rats as she did about The Nod and the crowd behind him. With loud cheers, the gallowglasses had hoisted him on their shoulders. He conducted the musicians and cracked jokes as he bobbed along.

"This is better than a birthday," said Frank, enjoying the excitement. His friends would never believe all this.

The sight of the bus threw the crowd into confusion. Some thought it was a castle and wanted to attack it. The mangonel tied behind was even more puzzling. Mary Kett explained all to Garrett and eventually he gave the order to board. There was a rush for the seats on the top and The Nod was enthroned up front.

"It looks very crowded. I do hope there's room for the Ancient Monuments," Mary Kett said to Garrett.

"Do we have to collect some old buildings?" he asked.

"Not quite," she said and explained about the passengers she hoped to collect in the town. She sat in the driver's seat, gritted her teeth and started the engine. Rex lay beside her out of harm's way. Momentary panic erupted at the noise of the engine starting.

"It's all right," roared The Nod and they believed him.

There was even more excitement when the bus increased speed. They had never travelled in a motor vehicle before. Garrett and the gallowglasses asked where all the woods had gone, as the country had many forests five hundred years before. They asked questions about everything.

"Where do you keep the horses?" Ruairí asked Mary Kett. He couldn't understand how the bus moved without them.

When they reached the main road they were amazed at the cars and trucks speeding past. This caused some panic but The Nod saved the day. In fact, he remained the soul of the party all the way to the town. He cheered and sang and the crowd on top joined in with him.

"Hey, look at that, men!" shouted Ruairí on seeing cattle in the surrounding fields. "We'll stop here on our way home!"

The thoughts of a cattle raid were never far from the mind of a gallowglass.

Miss Stitch and Firkin, the whippet, were standing at the head of the queue when the bus trundled up the street. They had got there early to make sure of a seat on the top. The remainder of the Ancient Monuments Society stood quietly in line behind. Firkin twitched at the sight of the overloaded singing bus and had lifted his leg against the lamp post three times before it pulled up. Mary Kett rolled down the driver's window and explained about the extra load on the top.

"They're friends of John's," she said. "He promised them a lift." Miss Stitch didn't look convinced, but was amazed as to how authentic their costumes looked.

"Disgraceful," she said. "There's hardly room on the top of the bus for Firkin and me."

"Never mind the rest of us," grumbled Bert the bank manager coming up behind her. Dressed as soldiers and maidens, the Ancient Monuments members filed onto the bus. The inmates from the cave didn't want to move over and there was jostling for places. Miss Stitch insisted on sitting on the top and dragged a leaking Firkin up the stairs. She wedged herself between two gallowglasses on the back seat and stayed put in spite of the terrible smell and their dangerous weapons.

She insisted, in no uncertain terms, that they remove their swords. The gallowglasses were delighted with this plucky lady and decided to humour her.

"Certainly, my beauteous wench," one said and nudged the other, who roared with laughter.

They unbuckled their swords and placed them in the back window. The largest gallowglass put his arm around her shoulders and insisted that she sing along with The Nod. She clammed up and glumly stared ahead. Firkin trembled and leaked under their feet.

Sadly, the situation didn't improve aboard the bus. The new arrivals muttered and mumbled about the cave people. Some agreed that it was better that they were on top because of the awful smell. Others complained that they couldn't get a view from the bottom. Mary Kett was driving a disgruntled and unhappy vehicle.

The fields on either side of road to the city had fine herds of cattle, quietly grazing in the sunshine. Unguarded cattle proved a great temptation to the gallowglasses. The lure was such that eventually a message was sent to Mary Kett to stop the bus.

"A call of nature," she thought, as she watched a gang from the top disappear behind the hedge. "Too much mead," she said to herself and settled back to wait.

A few moments later Miss Stitch wailed, "Why are those men chasing the cows around the field?"

Nobody seemed to know why.

Twenty cows were rounded up and driven onto the road in front of the bus. Ruairí told Mary Kett to move off.

"But the cattle are blocking the road!" she said, astonished.

"Drive them in front," Ruairí ordered.

Mary Kett protested that the cattle belonged to someone else but Ruairí was unmoved. He shrugged his shoulders and asked, "Who?" Two other gallowglasses joined him and glared at her fiercely.

When they drew their swords she decided to move on. Progress was slow as the cattle-driving was difficult. The cows often ran off and had to be collected and brought back.

"This is boring," Frank said to himself.

He thought that the bus would never get to the city in time for the parade. It was all very tiresome, the stopping and starting, people running after cows and the never-ending complaints. When the bus stopped for what seemed the fiftieth time and the gallowglasses jumped off to either chase or collect more cattle, he too stepped off.

To pass the time he walked slowly to the back of the bus and inspected the mangonel which was tied there. He climbed into the big spoon. He lay there, surprised at how comfortable it felt.

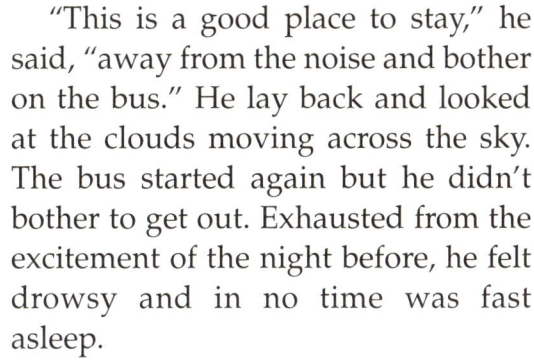

"This is a good place to stay," he said, "away from the noise and bother on the bus." He lay back and looked at the clouds moving across the sky. The bus started again but he didn't bother to get out. Exhausted from the excitement of the night before, he felt drowsy and in no time was fast asleep.

At first it seemed that nobody on the bus missed him. His mother, Mary Kett, had her own troubles. For her, the journey to the city was long and weary.

But Rex missed Frank and went searching for him. He couldn't find him but to his surprise discovered something even more interesting... Firkin. He had never seen such a strange skinny dog before. For a moment he was puzzled as to why the dog was sitting in a puddle until it dawned on him. It was a water dog! It stood to reason that a real water dog must sit in water. Delighted with his discovery, he barked a welcome. Firkin, unfortunately, thought that he was about to be attacked. He jumped out of his puddle and tore down the bus, spraying every seat as he ran past.

"So this is what a water dog does," thought Rex, who decided that he should do likewise. Following Firkin, he lifted his leg and sprayed the seats on the opposite side. Nobody seemed to notice, until Bert, the bank manager, jumped up shaking his foot.

"Firkin the Frenzied strikes again," he yelled. He launched a kick at the disappearing rump of Firkin who jammed himself under the nearest seat. Rex, too, dived for cover. The victims of the squirting dogs jumped up and shook their legs. It took some time for the uproar to settle.

"Nasty mongrel," growled Miss Stitch and lashed out at Rex as he scurried past. "Leading poor Firkin astray."

She set off down the bus, searching under the seats.

"Come to Mummy, Firkin dear," she cooed.

Mary Kett was relieved when they reached the suburbs of the city. The cattle refused to stop at traffic lights. The gallowglasses threatened any driver who blew at them. Eventually, they found a marching band and joined in behind. The band would take them to the start of the parade. Things got bad when the cattle, frightened by blaring horns, ran into gardens. Waving swords, the gallowglasses followed, frightening any unfortunate house owner who showed their face. As she steered her unruly bus through crowded streets, Mary Kett wished her husband would appear and rescue her from this mess.

CHAPTER NINETEEN

Breakout

The Museum of Natural History was surrounded by guards and soldiers when Garrett and John Kett arrived. The horses were very tired. Two flights in one night after five hundred years left them quite exhausted.

"Not before time," said Granny as the horses clattered onto the roof. "Strong can't hold out much longer."

Mrs Strong was indeed finding it hard to keep the cover on the roof-light. So fierce was the battering that she thought she was in danger of being launched into space. A huge crowd had gathered on the opposite side of the road. As far as they were concerned it was another film in the making. There were so many films being made these days that it was hard to guess which one this was.

"Definitely *Oliver Twist*," said one man. "It's the bit where they have poor Oliver on the roof towards the end."

"But I can't figure out the horses," a woman said.

"Did Black Beauty ever rescue Oliver Twist?" asked somebody.

"Isn't it marvellous how they make the horses fly."

"Probably rockets," said the first man.

Suddenly the roof-light cover flew upwards and Mrs Strong popped off the roof.

The crowd gasped as she dangled over the edge held only by the firehose.

"Climb back up," ordered Granny, "while we hold them off." The first head to appear through the roof-light was that of the Taoiseach.

"What's up with you?" Granny shouted. "Do you have to follow us everywhere?"

As he climbed onto the roof Granny rushed over, spun him around and gripped him in an arm lock. She pushed him towards the edge of the roof. Looking down, he trembled.

Two security guards popped their heads through the roof-light.

"One step nearer," Granny yelled. "And this thug goes over the side." A trembling Taoiseach tottered on the edge of the roof. He could see his firemen friends gathering below with the trampoline once again.

Mrs Strong had climbed up the firehose and was crawling across the slates.

"Quick, Granny," yelled James. "We have no time to lose."

He pushed Mrs Strong onto the horse behind Garrett.

Granny let go and the Taoiseach fell back onto the roof. As the guards poured across the roof and ran to help him, Granny was already running towards the horses.

James helped her onto the spare horse and climbed up behind her.

At a signal from Garrett the horses rose into the air or at least tried to rise into the air. Garrett and Mrs Strong's horse was stuck. Its hooves struck the air wildly but it couldn't move. It was firmly anchored to the roof.

"We forgot to untie the hose-reel," shouted John Kett.

The hose was still tied around the pipe where James had anchored Mrs Strong. The other end was still fixed around Mrs Strong. James tried to reach around her ample waist to untie the knot.

She was of no help as she wouldn't let go of the horse's mane.

"It's no good," he said, "I'll have to go back onto the roof and untie the hose."

"Wait," roared his dad. To their dismay they watched the Taoiseach run across the roof towards the pipe to which the hose was tied. He untied it and began to pull hard. He was trying to pull Mrs Strong off the horse!

"Help, I'm sliding off," yelled Mrs Strong. The Taoiseach pulled even harder. Garrett was sliding too.

"I have you at last," roared the Taoiseach.

James and Granny galloped towards them. As they passed by, he whipped the struggling horse on the flank. The horse snorted and spurted forward.

"Hold on tight!" Garrett shouted as the animal bucked and surged upwards. But the Taoiseach refused to let go. As the horse rose into the air, so also did the Taoiseach.

"Let go!" the guards shouted at him.

"Never!" he cried defiantly.

Holding on like grim death he sailed upwards behind Garrett and Mrs Strong.

The crowd on the pavement cheered at the sight of three airborne horses and a man hanging beneath them.

As they disappeared over the rooftops the man on the pavement said, "I don't remember this in *Oliver Twist*."

"Or in *Black Beauty* either," said the woman.

"It's never the same as the book," the man said and shook his head sadly.

Chapter Twenty
Granny to the Rescue

The Taoiseach was late. The guests were already sitting on the viewing stand. They glanced at their watches and looked up and down the street. As ever, it had been arranged that the Taoiseach should start the parade. The viewing stand was opposite the Post Office, the most important building in the wide street. The officials further down the street were finding it hard to hold back the crowd. There was a huge crush from behind. The St Macushla's High School marching band who were to lead off the parade were in trouble. There was a disturbance from somewhere behind.

The crowds were losing patience waiting for the start. Restless children ran onto the road. The guests on the stand craned their necks to spot the Taoiseach arriving. Only a small boy, perched high in a tree, saw him and the others land on the roof of the Post Office. The riders had been desperate to land somewhere, if it was only to get rid of the nasty shouting man tied to Mrs Strong. He hadn't stopped roaring since they left the Natural History Museum and he had almost pulled Mrs Strong off the horse.

"I'm pulled so tight around my middle, I can hardly breathe," she would scream.

"Hang on," James said. "Don't let him bug you." Garrett had wanted to cut the hose when they were flying across the Liffey but John Kett wouldn't hear of it.

Below them it was all confusion. People were milling around the streets and John Kett knew that the parade was about to start. As yet, he couldn't see the bus with Mary Kett and the Ancient Monuments.

"Land somewhere where we can watch the parade," James shouted.

"Anywhere to get off this horse," yelled Granny. "I'm saddle-sore."

"Anywhere to drop off this shouting thug," roared Mrs Strong. "I can feel last week's breakfast coming up."

The roof of the Post Office proved to be a good landing place. Two of the horses landed safely. As the third horse swooped down, the Taoiseach bumped off a large stone statue which stood at the edge of the roof. To save himself, he let go of the hosepipe, and threw his arms around the statue.

"Bedad, I'm slipping," he roared. He couldn't get a grip and slid downwards. Below him, between the porch pillars, hung long green banners which billowed gently in the wind.

At the sight of the Taoiseach wrapped around the statue, the crowd on the viewing stand rose to their feet.

"Wow!" they cried. "What a stunt!"

"Who is it?" someone asked.

"I bet it's Spiderman," said the boy in the tree.

"He looks familiar," the Lord Mayor said.

"Could it be the Taoiseach?" someone else asked.

"No, it couldn't. He's not wearing the coat."

"But he was due to arrive."

"What a way to arrive!"

As he slipped further the crowd began to applaud.

He couldn't stop now. He slipped past the statue and failed to catch the edge of the roof. As luck would have it the wind had caught one of the large green banners which had swelled out below. He grabbed the flag and hung suspended over the pavement.

"It must be Spiderman," the small boy said.

"It *is* the Taoiseach," someone in the crowd shouted.

"And without his coat," said the Lord Mayor.

"What a stunt!"

The television cameras along the street turned towards the building. Instantly, the Taoiseach appeared on every television set across the country.

Granny turned to Mrs Strong.

"They're calling him the Taoiseach."

"And we thought he was a thug," said Mrs Strong. "Lucky we didn't drop him in the river."

Granny thought for a moment.

"Where's the hose?"

"Tied around me," said Mrs Strong.

"Grab that statue," said Granny and as Mrs Strong obliged. Granny grabbed the loose end and carefully lowered herself over the edge of the roof. She worked her way down the face of the building to where the Taoiseach hung on the banner.

The crowd roared and the television cameras caught it all.

"Grab the hose, Taoiseach," Granny shouted.

"Never... you criminal hag!" he hissed. He forced a smile, mindful of the television cameras.

"We'll rescue you," Granny smiled. "Grab this hose and we'll pull you up." He glanced downwards. The pavement was a long way off. He imagined falling all that way, in full view of the television cameras. It wouldn't make good press to splatter onto the pavement. Reluctantly, he took the end of the hose.

"Clever," he thought. For the first time he felt a sneaking admiration for this troublesome woman.

Mrs Strong stood at the edge of the roof and began to twirl. As she spun, the hosepipe wound tight and Granny and the Taoiseach were pulled up. It was like being hauled up by a large revolving ballet dancer. At the top, John Kett and Garrett dragged them onto the roof. As they stood in a line between the statues, the crowd roared their approval. They held Granny's arm aloft as the television cameras relayed the event to the nation.

"A most successful venture," he thought. "The country will think me a hero for my display of courage." He smiled at Granny and said, "I have you, my good lady, to thank for this.

I must reward you in some way." Granny smiled sweetly, a glint in her eye.

Something was happening in the street below. The parade had finally started.

The loud noise of a siren made them turn in the opposite direction. The fire brigade was charging up the street, scattering the crowds. With a screech of brakes, it stopped on the road beneath them and the firemen jumped out. It was the same crew that rescued the Taoiseach before and they had come to save them again. They pulled out the trampoline and stood in the centre of the road. A ladder was pushed towards the top of the building.

"This is exciting," said Granny, who had never been rescued by a fireman and was quite looking forward to it.

Suddenly, they heard the sound of galloping hooves. The fire brigade men took to their heels. A herd of cattle came charging down the street, scattering the crowd for the second time. Guests on the stand screamed, fearing the worst.

"Goodness," said Granny. "If I'm not mistaken, those cattle are running amok."

CHAPTER TWENTY-ONE

Hearts and Minds

Granny wasn't mistaken. The cattle *were* running amok. Hard behind them ran the gallowglasses, fully intent on recapturing their escaped booty. The remains of St Macushla's High School band lay scattered along the street. The cattle had been heedless of their rendering of "Come Back to Erin" and had smashed right through. The crowd parted and the cattle disappeared down the street. To add insult to injury, the gallowglasses snatched the band's fallen instruments as they ran past following the cattle.

They considered these fair spoils. As Blossom O'Neill, their cheerleader from Brooklyn, New York, picked herself up from the gutter she wondered if the trip to the parade had been worth it.

The bus came into view, with The Nod perched up front. As rowdy as ever, he shouted at the fallen high school band members to "Ger' up outa' dat and join the party." Badly out of tune he sang, "Come Back to Erin". By the time they had reached the city, the entire bus was behind The Nod. He had so charmed them with his antics that, without exception, they would follow him anywhere.

The Taoiseach was annoyed to see that The Nod was still wearing his coat. He was further annoyed when the television cameras swung away from him and pointed at the singing Nod. There was a ripple of excitement from the crowd as they recognised the Taoiseach's secretary.

"We can't have that," the Taoiseach thought to himself. He was the one who should be on television, not The Nod.

"The fields are alive with the sound of music," he burst out singing. The others stared at him.

He continued singing as he climbed down the ladder, never taking his eye off the television cameras. He was again the centre of attention. On reaching the ground he suddenly stopped and his face became flushed. He had forgotten the rest of the words. He began to mumble.

"Hey looka dat!" someone shouted and the cameras moved back towards The Nod who was walking upside-down along the handrail on the bus.

"Drat," said the Taoiseach. "Gazzumped again."

The crowd applauded The Nod as he spun nimbly on the rail. He was now walking backwards. He smiled triumphantly towards the Taoiseach.

Granny and the others joined the Taoiseach on the ground. He looked dejected.

"It's the battle of the airwaves," he announced. "If The Nod wins the hearts and minds of the nation, it could be the ruin of me. Now that he's wearing my coat I might never be recognised again." He sobbed a little and Mrs Strong thought he looked a broken man.

"Never mind," said Granny, assuring him. "We can help."

"Can you really? " he almost pleaded.

She whispered with the others in a huddle and then turned to the Taoiseach.

"What will you give us if we win this competition for the minds and hearts of the nation?"

"Anything," sighed the Taoiseach, a desperate look in his eye.

Granny nodded and smiled to herself.

Meanwhile, The Nod had taken to blowing bubbles. He was marvellous. He blew bubbles within bubbles. He blew bubbles filled with smoke. He blew large bubbles, small bubbles, red, blue and green bubbles. The crowd loved it and cheered loudly. The cameras remained fixed on him until John Kett appeared on a bicycle from behind a large pillar.

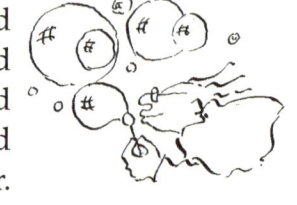

The Taoiseach stood on the saddle behind him, with his hands resting on his shoulders. They cycled into the centre of the roadway. The Taoiseach was back in the limelight. As they circled slowly, the Taoiseach raised one leg high into the air. The crowd yelled their approval. Then the Taoiseach cycled with his arms folded as John Kett balanced on the handlebars, his legs in the air. Their skill was remarkable. They were the darlings of the crowd and the television cameras until The Nod struck back.

The crowd parted and two horses complete with riders broke through. There was The Nod again, this time standing on the shoulders of two gallowglasses, each astride a horse. As the horses circled on the road, the gallowglasses stood up, raising The Nod even higher. The riders waved and disappeared behind the bus. The roar from the crowd was deafening. The Nod was one up again. The television cameras had followed them all the way.

"This won't do at all," said the Taoiseach.

"I'll have a go," said James, who decided he would demonstrate the exercises he had learned at his gymnastic class. He moved to the centre of the road where he thought that he would first present an "elephant stand". As he was trying to remember how it was done he heard a voice. "Move over, punk." It was his sister Joan.

Joan and Mary Kett appeared as a double skipping act. They sped along together, Mary twirling the rope. They circled a dumbfounded James. Fully behind The Nod, they had entered into the spirit of the competition.

"Traitors," hissed Granny as they passed.

"You lot started this first," Mary Kett shrugged as they vanished back through the crowd. The audience cheered. The television cameras waited for more.

"Juggle, Strong," ordered Granny. She piled four oranges into Mrs Strong's arms and pushed her into the centre of the road. Granny disappeared.

The cameras swung towards Mrs Strong, who attempted to juggle the oranges. She had never juggled before and surprised herself by letting only two oranges drop. But the crowd, expecting much better, was becoming difficult. The first "Boo" was heard, followed by shouts of "Butterfingers", and "Ger off". The television cameramen became bored and moved the cameras back towards the bus hoping for something better. Mrs Strong slunk off.

Things were looking bad for the Taoiseachs' team.

The onslaught from the opposition continued. A display of acrobatics and tumbling from Garrett's jester and servants set the crowd clapping.

As soon as they were finished, The Nod, Fingers, Mary Kett and Miss Stitch swung out onto the road. During the winter Miss Stitch had attended set dancing classes and, heedless of Granny, this was her chance to shine. Accompanied by Keenan on his harp, she and her pupils excelled themselves. They jigged over and back, up, down, in, out, over and under. Keenan was delighted. He hadn't had such an audience in five hundred years. The dancers finished to wild applause. Then came the fatal mistake.

Unfortunately for The Nod's team, Keenan decided to stay on. He sat with his harp in the centre of the road and began to sing his praise song to The Nod. This was the turning point. The crowd, delighted with the set dancing, found Keenan's dirge dismal. By the tenth verse the crowd became restless. By the twentieth they had become murderous.

"Put a sock in it," someone shouted.

Mrs Strong further incited the mob, by shouting,

"My budgie sings better,"

"Take him off,"

and,

"Shooting's too good for him."

"Who's killing the cat?" yelled James. The Nods' crowd was on the run now. If only Granny's gang had a good act to follow they would win the competition. But where was Granny? She was nowhere to be seen.

All at once the crowd rose and pointed at the top of the building. A rope had been strung from the base of the statue over the heads of the crowd. A solitary tightrope walker stood out against the sky.

With her skirt tucked in and holding a long pole to give her balance, Granny had stepped out onto the rope. She inched forward. The crowd held their breath. The fire brigade men ran to the centre of the road with the trampoline. As Granny edged along the rope, they moved with her. The crowd gasped as she wobbled a little, but then steadied. She slowly worked her way across the street until she reached the end of the rope. The fire brigade men stood directly underneath.

She gave a little hop and spun around, landing safely on the rope again. She faced back towards the building.

The crowd fell silent and waited. Tensely, the nation

watched on television. Dinners were burnt in a thousand ovens as cooks left their kitchens to view the spectacle in their living-rooms. There wasn't a cat to be seen on the streets of the country. The population sat huddled around their screens. Cars were abandoned along the roadside and motorists piled into public houses to watch the event on television. Flicking across his channels, the President of America picked up the event on satellite television. A traffic jam resulted on the streets of Tokyo when a huge crowd swelled around a television shop window.

Granny, unaware that she was the focus of world attention, stood staring down the rope. She nodded slowly. A figure emerged from behind the large statue. The Taoiseach, holding a balancing pole, stepped forward and placed one foot on the rope.

The crowd rose to their feet. The intake of breath could be clearly heard.

"Keep your eye on the rope and walk," shouted Granny from the other side of the street.

The Taoiseach obeyed and took another step. He quivered, but only for a moment. The President of America moved closer to his television screen. He telephoned the President of Russia and the television pictures were relayed on to him. Tokyo had ten traffic jams by this time.

The fire brigade men were in a terrible predicament as to who they should stand under. Finally, they ran to the centre of the road and stood ready to move in either direction. Granny and the Taoiseach inched towards each other. With every little wobble the fire brigade men ran over and back. They hoped to be in the right place at the right time.

Granny and the Taoiseach met in the middle of the rope.

"Ready?" Granny asked.

The Taoiseach nodded. Granny made another little hop and

spun around. She steadied.

"Now," she said and held her pole aloft. The world watched incredulously as, somehow, the Taoiseach climbed up and sat on Granny's shoulders. He held his balancing pole over his head.

Tokyo was by now at a complete standstill. The presidents of all the European states were glued to their television screens. The crowd on the street were completely silent except for The Nod and Ruairí who stood behind the bus. The Nod had taken Ruairí into his confidence and promised him even more booty if he would help him with his plan.

He growled at Ruairí. "My chance of becoming Taoiseach is slipping away fast."

"Barring an accident, of course," Ruairí quietly added and winked. "In the old days we would cut throats!"

The Nod ignored his last remark and said, "Perhaps – an accident!" Why didn't he think of that before. He looked around and then smiled. He had spotted the mangonel.

"Can you work this thing, Ruairí?" he asked.

Ruairí nodded. "Just unhook this rope."

"Let's have a bit of fun," The Nod suggested. "Why don't we fill the spoon thing with sweets and shower the crowd?"

"A good idea," said Ruairí with a laugh. The Nod disappeared. He filled some old sweetboxes full of bricks and stones and arrived back a few moments later.

"Shouldn't we take the sweets out first?" smirked Ruairí as The Nod pushed the boxes into the cradle.

"Oh, they'll open themselves, in the air," he replied as he turned the mangonel to point in the direction of the tightrope.

Frank woke up when two cardboard boxes full of stones and bits of brick were pushed on top of him. He was disappointed to find that the boxes were full of stones, not sweets. He had just pushed them back over the edge when he found himself flying through the air.

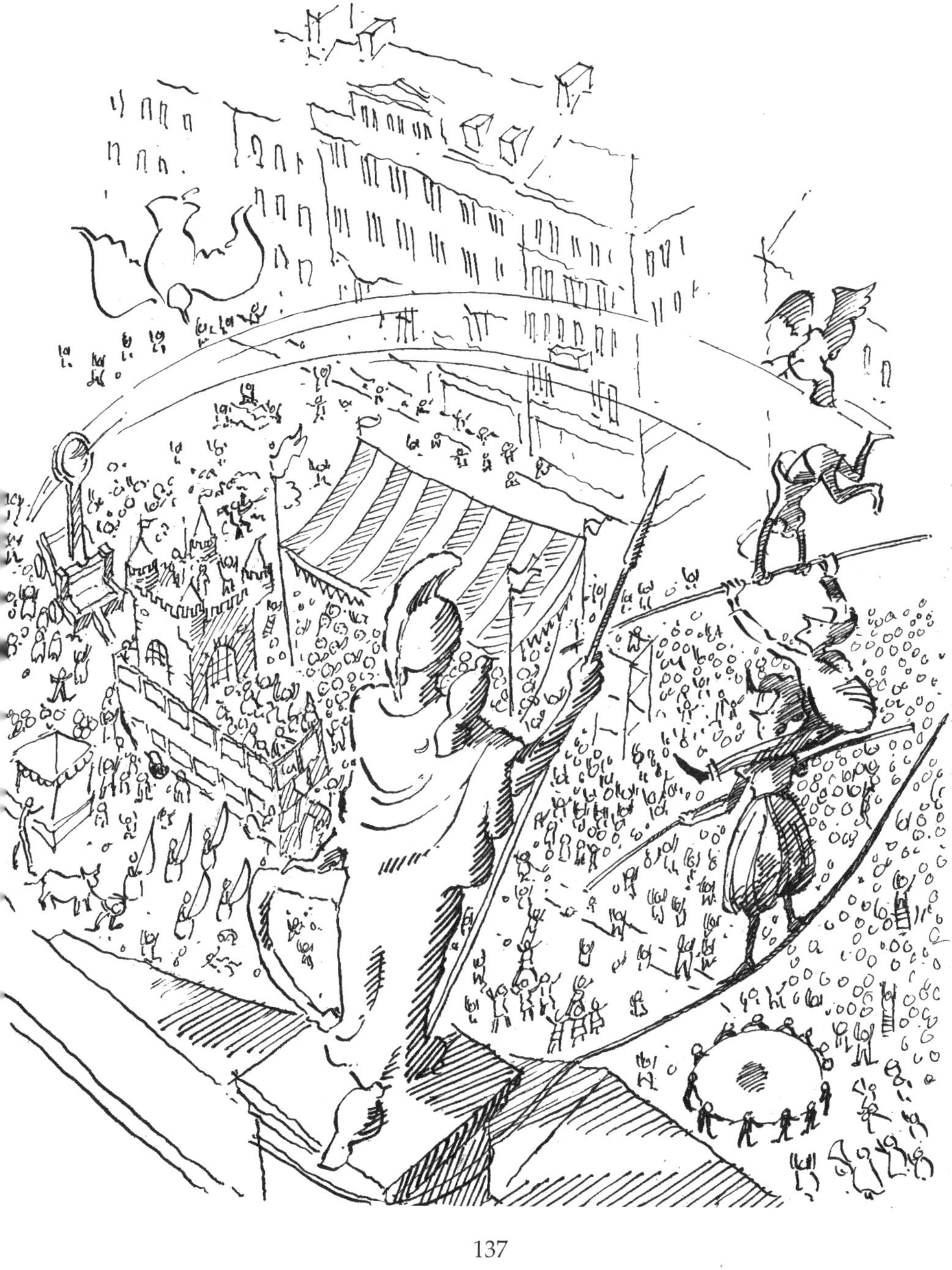

"Holy Moly," he shouted. He was spinning over the heads of a huge crowd and it was all happening so fast! Then he saw the tall man holding up the pole for him to catch.

"I wish people would tell me first," he cried as he grabbed the outstretched pole. He remembered the surprised look on the man's face as he swivelled over the pole and landed on the man's shoulders.

"Bedad!" shouted the man. "Where did you come from?"

Frank looked down and recognised his astonished grandmother staring up at him.

"Hello, Granny," he gasped as they all began to totter.

The flying Frank took Granny and the Taoiseach completely by surprise. When he landed on the Taoiseach's shoulders the world watched in stunned amazement. As they tottered over and back it held its breath. The fire brigade men danced below until they suddenly steadied.

Down below, Frank spotted his family among the crowd and waved. Joan wasn't impressed. "Show off," she mouthed from the ground.

The crowd remained silent as the high wire walkers inched their way back to the roof of the building. When Granny stepped onto the roof the cheers were deafening. The tightrope-walking trio bowed, smiled and waved. The nation applauded their television screens.

The cameras never turned to The Nod again. He was now a has-been. The Taoiseach's popularity was certain for the next ten years.

As they acknowledged the applause, the noise of bellowing came from down the street. Chased by the gallowglasses, the cattle were on the way back. Terrorised, the crowd scattered once again, to escape the stampede.

The street was in complete disorder. The viewing stand was abandoned, seconds before the cattle ran through it. Cushions, seats and planking were tossed high into the air. Important guests, hasty enough to think they could escape by climbing on to the bus, were pushed off by Miss Stitch. She manned the door and only let those aboard she recognised. Being short-sighted, very few got on. Garrett and John Kett just made it before she slammed the door shut. In the confusion of the moment Firkin the Frenzied had appeared at the bottom of the stairs. Mistaking him for Rex, Miss Stitch snarled "nasty mongrel" and booted him off the bus before slamming the door shut. It took him two weeks to find his weary and watery way home.

"Move it, Mary," John Kett shouted as he peered through the window at the riotous crowd. Mary Kett drove off at once, with the manic cows running alongside. She was delighted to leave the city and within an hour she was tearing along the road towards Hacklim.

CHAPTER TWENTY-TWO
All's Well

Granny, Strong, the Taoiseach, and James stood in the deserted street and looked after the bus. The Taoiseach was delighted. Thanks to Granny, he knew he had won the battle for the hearts and minds of the people. At that very moment their photographs were appearing on the front of every newspaper across the world.

Frank appeared with the Taoiseach's coat and glasses. From his perch on the tightrope he had seen The Nod drape them on a statue in the fountain called the "Floozy". Luckily the water was turned off at the time. The Taoiseach placed his glasses on his nose and examined his coat. He was clearly pleased to get it back. Even the greasy fingerprints, bubble marks and horse manure stains didn't dampen his delight.

"I'll deduct the cost of dry-cleaning from The Nod's wages," he said.

"Now, how can I reward you?" he asked Granny.

"Perhaps your gratitude is enough for me," Granny answered modestly, winking at Mrs Strong.

"No, I insist," he answered. "I promised you could ask me for anything!"

"Anything?" Granny asked innocently.

"Anything, gracious lady. Your wish is my command!"

Granny drew a deep breath.

"Then suggest me for the next President!"

There was a short silence as the Taoiseach drew himself up to his full height.

"An excellent idea. The country needs your sort of leadership. We will make an excellent pair."

James grinned at Granny as the Taoiseach added, "And besides it will stop that silly old bat from somewhere down the country writing to me every day about the job."

Granny smiled and winking at Mrs Strong said, "I bet you'll never hear from her again."

The Taoiseach seeing The Nod disappear into the parting crowd muttered gleefully, "I'll send The Nod as an ambassador to Outer Mongolia. Let him teach them to blow bubbles out there," he chuckled.

"In spite of it all, though, it has travelled well," he said, slipping the coat back on and sticking out his chest.

Granny thought that both the Taoiseach and the coat looked magnificent. Her heart skipped a beat as she reached out to touch it. The Taoiseach didn'tnotice.

"Watch your back, Taoiseach," thought Mrs Strong...

They all linked arms and strode up the street nodding and smiling at the home-going crowd.

The moon had already risen that evening when the bus arrived back in Hacklim. The Ketts were exhausted and said goodnight to the cave people.

"We'll call on you tomorrow," yawned John Kett.

Garrett looked a little sad. "It was a great adventure," he said. "I hope it will be as good next time I return."

Garrett was saying goodbye, although the Ketts didn't know it at the time.

They stood and watched him follow his people as they filed

across the hill. On the top he turned and waved. For a moment he stood out clearly against the moon. Then he disappeared.

In the days that followed they could never find the cave entrance again. Fingers said that they had all left that place and that the power was gone from the hill.

The children looked sad.

"Are they gone for good?" Frank asked sadly.

"No," said Fingers. "Other children will find them in another time or in a different place. They'll wait there until the country needs them again."

"Rubbish," thought Joan. "They must be in there." She resolved to find the way in herself.

But she never did. They moved back to the town soon after and quite forgot about Hacklim. After all, it was much more exciting to spend the summer visiting their Granny, the President.

£3.99

Age range: 8 – 12
Illustrated – 96 pages

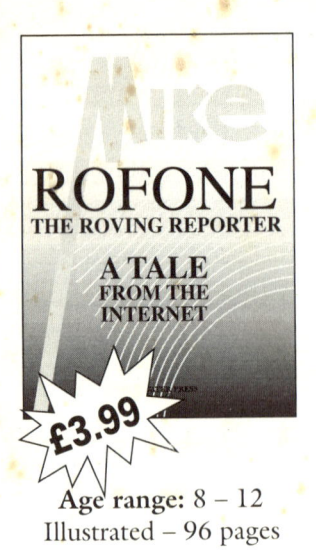

A story involving the Internet that moves along at the speed of a rollercoaster – with about as many twists and turns.
No knowledge of the Internet required!

£3.99

Age range: 8 – 12
128 pages

A fast-moving story of how three young teenagers tackle all obstacles with courage, ingenuity and humour.

Order 1 book – £3.50, 2 books – £6.50, 3 books – £8.50

£3.99

Age range: 8 – 12
128 pages

Ignatius proves to be as charming a pig as 'Babe' in this captivating and original tale.

Special discount offers

Order Form

Send your order (with this page or a copy) plus cheque to:
BLACKWATER PRESS CHILDREN'S BOOK OFFER
c/o Folens Publishers, Unit 7/8 Broomhill Business Park, Broomhill Road, Tallaght, Dublin 24.

I wish to order: Mike Rofone ☐   Reaching The Heights ☐   Ignatius The Wonderful Pig ☐

I enclose a cheque for £ .... (includes post and packaging)

Name: ....

Address: ....

....

Telephone: ....

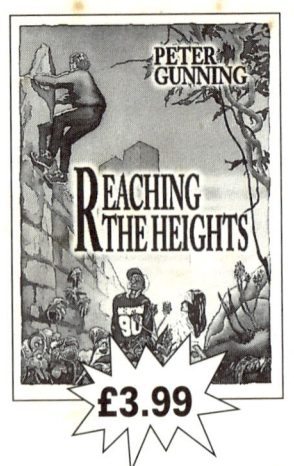